DAYBREAK ON NEW

Night-quiet, the two assassins advanced—like shadows unseen in the overlying murk and as deadly as the wind-spiders of the western tundra. Just ahead Gunnar, the contracted victim, ran, ignoring the pain that constricted his chest and stabbed in his lungs. He ducked instinctively as the Khaelian-made dagger creased him in a burning line from shoulder to mid-back, then slipped and fell in the rank mud at his feet.

The Hoorka assassins stood over him. Gunnar lay face down in the mud, waiting for the cold rape of steel to pierce his body. But relays warned them that morning had touched the Dawnrock with delicate fingers. It would be so easy to kill Gunnar despite the Hoorka code. No one was there to see . . .

Strong hands helped Gunnar to his feet, grunting with the man's limp weight.

"Our admiration, Gunnar. Your life is your own once more," the Hoorka said in a voice that masked his bitterness. "You may go with the light."

SLOW FALL TO DAWN

Stephen Leigh

BANTAM BOOKS
TORONTO · NEW YORK · LONDON · SYDNEY

SLOW FALL TO DAWN
A Bantam Book / October 1981

ISBN 0-553-14902-4

Published simultaneously in the United States and Canada

Bantam Books are published by Bantam Books, Inc. Its trademark, consisting of the words "Bantam Books" and the portrayal of a rooster, is Registered in U.S. Patent and Trademark Office and in other countries. Marca Registrada. Bantam Books, Inc., 666 Fifth Avenue, New York, New York 10103.

PRINTED IN THE UNITED STATES OF AMERICA

0 9 8 7 6 5 4 3 2 1

for DENISE—
she knows why,
but still enjoys being told

SLOW FALL
TO
DAWN

One

Pause. And shiveringly inhale. The two Hoorka-kin gathered air for their complaining lungs. It had been a long run for Aldhelm and Sartas, far too long. Sweat varnished the skin under their nightcloaks, and their legs were cramped and sore. Still, the quarry was just ahead, and they could allow themselves only the briefest rest. Night-quiet, the two assassins advanced like shadows unseen in overlying murk; as deadly as the wind-spiders of the western tundra.

In but seventeen minutes, the photoreceptors on the dawnrock would signal Underasgard's dawn and the end of their hunt. They ran, the Hoorka.

Aldhelm signaled Sartas to a halt in the comforting darkness cast by a high porch. Somewhere just ahead, Gunnar—the contracted victim—was enmeshed in the thick metal pilings that held the houses above the early rains and the cold flood that inevitably followed. These were the tenements of Sterka, the most temporary sector of a city that had not been meant by its founders to survive more than half a century and was now well into its second hundred of years. Wooden beams lent support to the time- and rust-weakened pillars of metal. Decay, an odor formed of river mud and rust, filled their nostrils. Aldhelm fought the inclination to cough in the fetid air.

It hadn't been an easy or lucky night for them.

The apprentices had done their work admirably. With six hours still to pass before the Underasgard dawn terminated the contract, Aldhelm and Sartas had taken up the trail within meters of Gunnar. They'd pursued him down the Street of Ravines, scenting an easy kill and an early night; the Thane would be pleased, for this was politically an important assassination. The street was deserted, the only light coming from hoverlamps spaced at long intervals, and Gunnar was already winded. But as the Hoorka reached for their daggers, Gunnar suddenly lifted his head, cast a frightened yet oddly hopeful look behind him, and ducked into a cross street to his left. A moment later, the two Hoorka heard the sound that had caused Gunnar's optimism —the low-moaning chant of the Dead, a lassari sect. The Dead were the disenfranchised, the most depressed of the unguilded, the lassari. Their balm was ignorance, their unity hopelessness. Those of the Dead did nothing save to march and chant their melancholy mantras, accompanied by the scent of burning incense and finding cartharsis in the act of marching. Their indifference to reality was legendary; the Dead paid no attention to pedestrians in their path, ignored the occasional assaults on peripheral members of their processions, and failed to notice their own members who would swoon and fall from exhaustion. They considered their lives already ended. Why should any lagging pain from the life they considered finished bother them? They marched to meet Hag Death, and took her foul embrace as they would that of a lover.

The Dead entered the Street of Ravines from the right of the cross street, and made a slow, agonizing turn toward the Hoorka. There were perhaps thirty of them, eyes closed as they chanted, their bodies—wrapped in simple cloth robes—filling the narrow street. Cursing, the Hoorka fought to make a passage through the press. The fuming censers filled their nostrils with acrid fumes, and around them the expressionless faces moved in the sibilant chanting, ignoring the Hoorka who pushed and shoved the unresisting Dead from their path. Aldhelm raised an open hand—the Dead One on his left was a young woman who looked as if she might have once been pretty—and pushed her away from him. Her eyes opened briefly, though she didn't look at him, and then she resumed her chanting, stumbling as she regained her balance.

And abruptly, they were through. The procession of Dead, unruffled, continued down the street, their chant echoing from the buildings to either side. Gunnar had disappeared. The Hoorka ran down the cross street, searching the alleyways that led off from the street. Dame Fate rewarded their diligence. Aldhelm motioned to Sartas, beckoning. He gave inward thanks to She of the Five Limbs for her favor, and moved into a narrow, dingy alley.

The moons were yet to rise, but a pallid lemon light filtered through a greasy window high up on one wall of the bordering structures. The window gave but a wan and uncertain illumination, but with the light-enhancers the Hoorka wore, it was enough. They could see Gunnar, halfway up a pile of packing crates that had been thrown into the alley, blocking it. Gunnar hadn't yet seen the Hoorka, but in his haste to get by the crates, he sent them tumbling noisily to the ground. Sartas grinned at Aldhelm and loosened his vibro in its sheath. A victim so obviously frightened, so careless, was an easy kill.

But his very clumsiness saved Gunnar. The lighted window was suddenly flung open. Brilliant light washed over the alley, stabbing at the packing crates, the startled Gunnar, and the cobbled surface of the ground.

"Bastard!" a voice shouted, hoarsely. "Get away from those crates or I'll have your manhood!"

Gunnar whirled, losing his precarious balance and sending more crates to the ground. He slipped, tumbling halfway to earth, and in that instant saw the Hoorka, momentarily blinded by the sudden overload of the light-enhancers. Sartas flung his vibro: a wild throw, it came nowhere near Gunnar. And as the Hoorka recovered their vision and moved toward their victim, the window was slammed shut again with a final curse. In the time it took the Hoorka to regain sight once more, Gunnar scrambled over and through the labryinth of crates and into the maze of streets beyond.

Sartas picked one of the cobblestones from the alley, hefted it, and sent it crashing through the window.

"May all your children be lassari," he shouted. "And if your pride is offended by my insult, see Sartas of the Hoorka. I'll give you satisfaction *and* an introduction to Hag Death."

Silence. After a moment, Sartas grinned. "He doesn't answer, Aldhelm. Too bad."

Aldhelm didn't share his companion's humor. "We have to find Gunnar, kin-brother. This is petty."

"Let's go, then."

They found Gunnar again more because the apprentices had done their preliminary work than through any skills of their own. Gunnar's mistress, Ricia Cuscratti, lived in the Burgh. As with most neighborhoods in Sterka, the rich lived in uncomfortable proximity to the poor, and m'Dame Cuscratti, a member of the Banker's Guild, was rich. The Hoorka, having little recourse, made their way to her dwelling after ascertaining that Gunnar had fled in that direction.

The Cuscratti house was large, set away from the street and buffered by a well-lit garden. Parti-colored hoverlamps flickered above the topiary and illuminated the skeleton of a small ippicator. The wall facing the street was translucent —colors melted and collided in abstract patterns while the shadows of figures moved in the rooms behind. Aldhelm and Sartas paused, taking refuge in the shadowed recesses of a run-down warehouse adjacent to the house.

"We could wait for him." Sartas's voice was heavy with his breathing.

Aldhelm, in darkness, shook his head. "There isn't that much time now. No, *if* he's there, he'll stay unless we set him running again. We'll have to go in."

"As you say." Sartas shrugged. "I'll want hot mead when we get back to the caverns. If Felling doesn't have the cooking fires lit, I'll use his bed for kindling."

It took no great skill to loose the hoverlamps from the magnetic field powering them. The lamps fell like stunned fireflies, and in darkness the garden gave more cover than they required. The flowing colors of the wall cast oddly-hued shadows from the trimmed shrubbery. Drifting patches of shade twisted like pastel vines over the street and into the houses beyond. Aldhelm and Sartas were quickly standing near the doorshield. Aldhelm rummaged in his nightcloak, found the random field generator, and began to adjust the device, searching for the frequency that would dilate the shield and let them pass. The mechanism hummed loudly in the quiet of the garden.

In the night silence, the Hoorka heard the footsteps many seconds before anyone came into view. The assassins slipped into deeper cover and watched four men approach the house from the street. The figures hesitated near the entrance to the garden, and the wall threw mad images dancing behind them, animating the sleeping hulks of buildings. The intruders made no attempt at stealth, nor did they bother with any subtlety when confronted by the obstacle of the doorshield. One of the four brought a fieldgun to bear. Phosphorescent sparks arced, spat angrily, and expired on the rich humus of the garden. The translucent wall rippled patterns of alarm: billows of purple-scarlet welled outward from the shield and spread across the face of the house, growing larger and more saturated with color. Somewhere inside, a disconsolate siren wailed mournfully and shadow-figures raced from front to back, away from the disturbance. The intruders—Aldhelm could see them clearly in the aching blue-white glare of the dying shield—wore cloaks not unlike the gray and black nightcloaks of the Hoorka-kin, but these were no Hoorka. He signaled to Sartas, using the hand code. *Vingi's people?*

In the depths of some fanciful bird of shrubbery, Sartas's hand moved in reply. *Probable.*

A flick of a hand, a flashing of palm. *We'll wait.*

The shield died in orange and white agony. Flame guttered and died, running fitfully up and down the perimeter of the opening as the door dilated. The four ran quickly past the smoking ruin and into the house, weapons ready. Aldhelm unsheathed his vibro.

Now. Aldhelm nodded to Sartas, and the two Hoorka swept past the wreckage of the shield.

They were in a reception room. An animo-painting swirled on the far wall and ornate floaters waited for occupants. Lifianstone pillars carved like vines climbed from floor to distant ceiling in a mockery of nature, curling and spreading when they reached the balcony that overlooked the room. Beyond the balcony, the Hoorka could hear the sounds of a struggle, and then the wall opposite the railings began to smoke as a line of blistering paint ran quickly across it in a ragged diagonal. A hand laser, then. The thought did little to comfort Aldhelm. Standing in the room, they were exposed to anyone caring to glance over the balcony rail.

Aldhelm moved to the staircase (carved mermen waved flippered hands at carved fish in a frozen ocean: the railing), and Sartas followed quickly. They ran quietly up the stairs.

"I don't like this. We're not armed or protected for a laser fight." Aldhelm glanced back at Sartas.

"*You* want to go back and explain all this to the Thane? This would be a cleaner death."

"He's going to be upset no matter what happens." Aldhelm exhaled deeply. "Dame Fate keeps playing Her hand against us tonight, and I don't like that."

Aldhelm crouched down and glanced around the corner at the top of the staircase. Nothing. "Fine," he said. "Let's find out who these fake guild-kin of ours are."

This floor of the house was built in a semi-circle around an interior garden redolent with tropical flowers. Across the open space, Aldhelm could see the focus of fighting. The four cloaked men had taken shelter behind a convenient sculpture and were firing into a darkened archway that led further back into the interior of the house. Someone was returning their fire with a projectile weapon. Aldhelm could hear the whine of shells and see chunks of masonry flying as the bullets struck the walls. The Hoorka began moving to one side of the battle.

"Damned clumsy people, these counterfeit Hoorka," muttered Sartas.

"They're not particularly alert. We could take them easily enough. Go around to the left. I think we can circle the garden and come out somewhere on the other side of that arch."

"They've enough firepower to destroy the house. Clumsy."

"Yah," Aldhelm agreed. "But let's stay out of their way. If we can get around them, maybe we can get to

Gunnar first. I don't like the thought of someone's blood-feud interfering with our contract."

They had no chance. There was a sudden flurry of movement as three of the intruders rushed the archway while the other kept his laser activated and pointed at the corridor beyond. Then the three were past the arch and the sound of a physical struggle intensified. A high scream like tearing velvet rose and died. The last of the intruders ran through the archway. The Hoorka waited.

Nothing.

Aldhelm strode quickly across the garden, heedless of the painstakingly-arranged plants he was trampling underfoot, and Sartas followed. At the archway, they paused, peering inside cautiously. A purplish fog filled the corridor and wisped about the lamps set in the wall. A woman's body, wrapped in a gauzy dress, lay on her side, crumpled against the wall with an odd lack of blood. The intruders were gone. Aldhelm gestured to Sartas to stay, and went to examine the body. He turned it over gently—it was Ricia. He didn't need to check the pulse to know that she was in Hag Death's domain.

The Hoorka followed the path of the intruders through the house—the trail of a running battle. Here were charred draperies, there a vase overturned and broken. They passed through a series of bedrooms, an expansive dining area where a stray bolt had evidently hit a power circuit and dumped the table, set for dinner, onto the floor. Silver utensils littered the tiles, slivers of crockery crunched underfoot. They went through a kitchen, then were back outside again. And when they found themselves out of the grounds and back in the entangling clustering of houses, they came upon an apprentice Hoorka waiting for them, out of breath.

"The Thane sent me, sirrahs." A gasping intake of breath, fish-mouthed. "He has learned that Vingi (breath) has sent some of his guard (breath) force to kill Gunnar."

Aldhelm and Sartas glanced at each other, then Aldhelm grimaced and nodded. "So Vingi doesn't trust the task to Hoorka. Well, he's managed to foul it up for himself. We have to track Gunnar again."

The apprentice clutched his sides and crouched

slightly. "I saw Gunnar leave this house as I came here," he said as he straightened. "He began moving toward the river, and he seemed to know the ground well. Vingi's guards—at least I assume the men I saw were of the Li-Gallant Vingi's guild—had a short meeting in the garden near the ippicator skeleton. They left in the direction of Vingi's keep."

Sartas shook his head at Aldhelm. "I told you they were incompetent." The Hoorka chuckled.

"The Thane won't be laughing if we fail to meet the contract." Aldhelm turned to the apprentice. "Tell the Thane that we've already had a problem with Vingi's guard. You can also tell him—but step back when you do so—that Gunnar is still alive. Then run, neh?"

The apprentice grinned and nodded. He bowed his salutation to the Hoorka and was off. The sound of his running could be heard for some time in the sleeping city.

That had been hours ago. Now they were finally in sight of Gunnar again, having tracked him through the twisting streets. Aldhelm could see the man clearly. Gunnar was breathing heavily, his right arm extended as he leaned against the understructure of the tenements. His head was bowed, his knees were slightly bent. The muck of the river had caked his shoes—he'd been easy to follow since entering undercity.

The ooze glistened coldly with slats of blue-white light. The seams of the flooring overhead grinned with age. Aldhelm could hear the indistinct rise and fall of murmured conversation above him, punctuated unevenly with the breathing of Sartas and himself. A voice complained loudly of the abundance of sandmites as the Hoorka began moving.

The mud that had so clearly marked this stage of Gunnar's flight also aided him. Even Hoorka assassins, adept at silentstalk, were not immune to chance, as this night had amply proved. The river-filth sucked greedily at the soles of their boots, relinquishing them with a liquid protest. Gunnar's head snapped up: they were still thirty meters from him, under the next dwelling. The man ducked instinctively, and the Khaelian-made dagger only creased him, drawing a burning line from shoulder to mid-back before burying its ultra-hard point several millimeters into the metal pillar behind him. Even as Gunnar looked up, weighing the chances of grasping the dagger, it began to wriggle and loosen, the electronic devices in the dagger seeking to return to the homing pulse from the Hoorka. Gunnar floundered to his feet and ran, weaving from pillar to pillar.

(And Aldhelm cursed under his breath, reproaching the Goddess of Chaos for tipping the scales of chance so unequally, and praying that She of the Five would hold back the sun—dawn at Underasgard would give Gunnar his life.)

The Hoorka knew Gunnar would be praying to his own gods for the light, for Underasgard was but fifty kilometers distant and the sun would touch the dawnrock at much the same time as dawn here in the city of Sterka. Then —unmoved and uncaring, at least outwardly—the Hoorka would be bound to let the man live. Already the morning sky was luminous with that promise.

Aldhelm, knowing this, sought to end it quickly.

He loosed another dagger. It clattered from a pillar and, twirling, struck Gunnar handle foremost. Silver glimmered as the weapon turned and arced back to the Hoorka.

Pursuer and pursued ran, ignoring the banded pain that constricted their chests and stabbed in their lungs. Sartas threw: the dagger found a pillar at Gunnar's right, and the man feinted left and dove as another Hoorka blade fountained mud at his feet. Gunnar slipped, coating himself with umber goo, and regained his footing. The stench of decaying vegetation made him gag, and he slipped again, retching and struggling. Mud blinded him. He scrabbled frantically at his face.

The Hoorka stood over him. Gunnar lay in the mud, and Aldhelm watched the man flailing in panic, knowing Gunnar could feel the pressure of his gaze, knowing the man was waiting for the cold rape of a blade piercing his body, twisting deep into his entrails . . .

But the relays had told them that morning had touched the dawnrock with its delicate fingers. Aldhelm looked about him. It would be so easy to kill Gunnar despite the Hoorka code. No one would see, and it might save future trouble with Li-Gallant Vingi. He sighed, glancing at Sartas, weighing the choices in his mind. Sartas shook his head, sensing Aldhelm's hesitation.

Dawn was a tepid light on a misty morning. They helped Gunnar to his feet, grunting with the man's limp weight.

"Come on, damnit. You can stand." Aldhelm's voice was neither ice nor fire, not devoid of emotion but rather so full of it that the individual nuances were indistinguishable with surfeit.

The Hoorka watched composure slowly return to Gunnar's drawn, haggard face. He wiped vainly at his soiled clothing, looking as if he were about to speak. But he lowered his eyes and looked at the ruin of his pants.

Aldhelm spoke again. "Our admiration, Gunnar. Your life is your own once more." His voice, without the inflections that might have turned it mocking and bitter, spoke of the ritualistic completion of a ceremony. "You may go with the light."

"Ricia's dead." Gunnar's voice was cracked and dry; his eyes were wild, puzzled.

"M'Dame Cuscratti was not killed by Hoorka. That is a matter of bloodfeud between yourself and another. You will bear the truth of that." For a moment, Aldhelm's eyes glinted angrily in the dawnlight, then he half-turned. "Make your way home. Your path is safe," he said. Aldhelm motioned to Sartas, and the assassins were gone, slipping into the twilight gloom of undercity.

Gunnar stood: dripping and covered with filth, gasping with tortured lungs, confused and thankful both. He glanced at the landscape around him, then stared at the ruddy arc of sun above the line of trees across the river. He breathed deeply and walked away.

The house stood well away from the river and its urban banks. Unlike the majority of Neweden buildings, this one disdained the pillared, flighty architecture, and squatted dourly on the earth, attended by a cluster of outbuildings. It straddled the crest of a low hill that was the first outcropping of the Dagorta Mountains, and it was similar to the other dwellings of this fertile land in that it too had ranks of gardens and trees shielding the Neweden soil from the sunstar. Sterka, the city, lay in blue-tinged distance, just visible from the highest point of the rise: the city was a massive grouping of buildings, with the outlying burghs arrayed before it like a shield, a buffer against the wilderness. As a panorama, the view wasn't exceptional—the most common scenes of a hundred worlds of the Alliance were more pleasing aesthetically, and Neweden herself had better, but it satisfied those who normally dwelt here. It reeked of sylvan, pastoral quietness. Unassertive, it seemed strong.

Through this display of verdant order, a man moved, stumbling and slow. His hair was matted and gleaming with sweat, his tunic torn and coated with mud now dried and caked to a sienna lamination. He walked clumsily, drunkenly, nearly falling now and again, as if he weren't fully awake or aware of his surroundings. The sun glazed the air about him, and drone-beetles made desultory circles about his head, flying lazily away with every step. He raised his head to stare at the cluster of buildings on the rise, focusing his attention on the main house with its mirror walls reflecting the heat-wave of the guard shield around it. The windows were opaqued and empty. He stood, as the sun inched itself infinitesimally higher in the cloud-choked sky, and some animal hooted disconsolately in the nearby woods. Then he lowered his head and resumed his ambling, slow progress toward the crest.

He reached the guard shield and halted again. He stared at the house, his hand shielding his eyes from the reflected sun-glare as the walls threw back the image of his surroundings. Nothing moved, nothing acknowledged his arrival. Shrugging—dried mud fell from the sleeve of his tunic to the ground, revealing purple cloth—he placed his hand on the butler post and let it scan his fingerprints. The guard shield coalesced and drew back from the butler, leaving him room to pass through an opening defined by a sparking perimeter. He moved through and onto the manicured lawn beyond.

"A good morning, sirrah," the butler said as the shield collapsed back into position. The man didn't reply. After a pause, the post spoke again. "Sirrah Potok will be glad to see you."

"No doubt he told you to expect me." The man's voice was weary.

A moment's silence as the butler scanned its small memory. "I'm afraid not, sirrah. You, of course, are always welcome here. Should I inform the house?"

But he'd already moved on. The butler, uncaring, lapsed into silence.

He performed the same ritual at the door, placing his hands before the entry plate and allowing the mechanism to identify and clear him. The door dilated silently, and he was inside.

The room he entered was small and made even more claustrophobic with furniture and racks of books and microfiche. He sighed, taking in the familiarity, allowing himself to relax for the first time that day. The same flat paintings, the well-used and scarred malawood desk with flimsies scattered over it in a paper avalanche, the holotank stolid in isolated dominance in the center of the room, floaters arranged before it for an invisible audience: all of this evoked calm and comfort. Home.

From the meeting room just beyond the archway to his right, he could hear the basso, garbled drone of filtered and shielded speech. He moved toward the sound, pushing open the intricately-carved doors.

"*Gunnar!*"

Potok, rotund and florid, his minister's garb in its habitual disarray, rose from his seat at the head of a long table. The four remaining people in the room looked up in surprise, glancing first at the astonished face of Potok and then following his eyes to where Gunnar stood, leaning against the door. Potok shook his head and one pudgy hand went to smooth non-existent hair. He spoke with obvious relief in his voice.

"Gunnar," he repeated. "I don't believe this. We thought—" he broke off his speech and came around the table. With a guttural obscenity, he took Gunnar's hand, then clasped him fully. Gunnar managed a wan smile.

"By all the ippicators in hell, man, you stink." Potok held Gunnar at arm's length and looked down at the mud that now smeared his own clothing. "Where've you been crawling?"

"I'd rather not think about it." Gunnar's grin wavered and died as the color drained from his face. He ignored the others in the room—guild-kin, all members of his own ruling guild—looking at Potok with eyes quickly moist and fragile. His gaze darted about, without seeing anything, from the table ringed with moisture from glasses to the faces staring at him to the empty, black windows. "Potok," he said, with discernable effort in his voice, "they killed Ricia. I saw it."

"Ricia? Who, the Hoorka?"

"No, some others." Gunnar remembered the Hoorka's eyes. *M'Dame Cuscratti was not killed by Hoorka,* he'd said. *You will bear the truth of that.* And Gunnar understood the implicit threat in those words. "I don't know who they were, unless that bastard Vingi sent them. They weren't Hoorka, at least I don't think so . . ." His voice trailed off as he seemed to notice the others for the first time. "Sirrahs Tuirrene, de Vegnes, Hollbrook, m'Dame Avina." He nodded to each in turn. "I'm sorry to have to bear such tidings to my kin. I, umm, don't . . ."

He turned back to Potok. "I'm just tired, too tired." He shook his head and took a slow breath. "I seem to have interrupted a meeting of the Guild Council. Have I disturbed something of importance?" Gunnar looked at m'Dame Avina, but she seemed intent on studying a chip on the side of her mocha cup.

"Gunnar?" Potok's voice brought Gunnar's head around sharply. "We were meeting to discuss the future of our guild, to elect a new kin-lord."

"You couldn't wait? You couldn't take the time to know that I'd been killed? Is that what you're saying, my friend?" Gunnar's voice held an edge that cut all of them.

"No one here thought you'd escape the Hoorka."

"You didn't seem upset when I decided to run rather than remain here. And had you elected the new head?" Scorn lashed them.

"We"—Potok glanced back at the others—"hadn't yet come to a decision."

"Then I'm sorry to have interrupted you with such

alarming news." As if he could no longer sustain his anger, Gunnar slumped, leaning heavily against the wall. He closed his eyes for a long moment, then opened them again. "I have to rest. There's much we have to do. With Ricia gone."—the pain returned briefly to his face—"we have no contacts among the upper strata of Sterka. Discuss that, if you must plot and plan. And send someone to see Ricia's guild-kin and offer our support, to make sure that all the rites are performed for her, until I can see to it myself." He paused, and the room seemed to waver before him. "I need a bed," he said, simply.

"Upstairs. Your normal room." Gunnar, with Potok's help, took his leave. At the door to the bedroom, Gunnar paused and sighed. "My legs ache like hell." He shook his head, started a laugh tinged with hysteria, then shook his head again.

Potok opened the door for him and took his arm. "I *am* glad to see you again, Gunnar."

"Despite any thwarted ambitions?"

"You taught me ambition. If I've learned too well, you can only blame yourself. And with the Hoorka contract, it was easy to think of you as . . . dead." Potok shrugged. "The guild would have declared bloodfeud when the Hoorka revealed the signer of the contract. You would have had your revenge, and the gods would have been at rest."

"A small compensation, I suppose. And I did enjoy the guilt on your faces when I entered. Tell me, Potok, who had you elected?"

Potok stared at Gunnar, his eyes challenging. "Myself. But I step down gladly now that you're back." A pause. "Truthfully."

"I'll sleep easier for that knowledge." Gunnar nodded his thanks to Potok and closed the door.

On his way downstairs, Potok wondered if it had been sarcasm or merely weariness in Gunnar's voice.

Two

The Hoorka-thane was possessed by the closest approximation of rage any had ever seen in him. The Thane found himself very aware of Sondall-Cadhurst Cranmer, watching from a floater near the thermal duct behind the Thane. He knew the man, the little scholar, would be alternately fascinated and frightened by the outburst, and that he would be busily recording the new facets of the Thane's personality that this outrush of temper revealed.

That knowledge did nothing to quell the irritation. The Thane faced Aldhelm and Sartas, his face lined with emotion. "Gunnar simply escaped, you say. Unarmed. Alone." The words fell like hammer blows. "The two of you let him live until dawn. Two supposedly competent Hoorka let simple prey escape them?" The Thane's voice was laced with mock surprise that raked Aldhelm and Sartas. The Hoorka bore the outburst in obedient silence.

The Thane gestured with a fisted hand. "Do both of you need training in rudimentary exercises? I won't permit this, not now. I won't have Hoorka destroyed by incompetence. You, Aldhelm." In a swirling of nightcloak, the Thane turned and glared at him. "You're the best knife man of our kin. How could you have missed, how could you have allowed this to happen?"

Aldhelm and Sartas looked at the Thane, though neither one moved nor spoke. His last words came redundantly back at them, an echo from the far walls of the cavern in which they stood. Hoverlamps glistened from water-filmed rocks and ruddied their complexions, making deep hollows of their eyes. Underasgard. Hoorka-home. The caverns. Again the Thane was conscious of Cranmer watching from his vantage point, and he remembered that once the scholar had made the comparison between the Thane and the caverns: both cool, dark, and with hidden recesses you felt more than saw. And one more thing that he hadn't said. Old.

A vibroblade gleamed in the Thane's hand, the luminous tip describing short lines of brilliance in the atmosphere of the cavern—the Thane had brought them away from the well-lit rooms of the main caverns, not wanting to admonish the two Hoorka in public. Vibro held foremost, the Thane advanced upon them. They didn't flinch.

"Do the two of you realize what you've done? When I came to Neweden there were no Hoorka, only a band of petty thugs without kinship; lassari, no more respect than the processions of the Dead. I spent years setting up our guild, gaining us grudging respect, making this a group protected by the Neweden Assembly and tolerated by the Alliance. Idiots!"

The blade swept before their eyes. The following wind cut them coldly. Cranmer—the Thane saw him at the edge of his peripheral vision—jumped involuntarily, but the two Hoorka before the Thane stood in taut rigidity.

"The Li-Gallant Vingi himself signed that contract," the Thane continued. "Gunnar's death would have left the opposing Ruling Guild in shambles—and Vingi might have had total control of the Assembly. Don't you see the possibilities there? Fools!"

The Thane gesticulated violently and the vibro tip gashed Aldhelm's cheek. Blood, bright scarlet, ran freely, but Aldhelm didn't grimace or show pain beyond a narrowing of his eyes. The Thane cursed himself inwardly: he shouldn't have drawn blood then, shouldn't have let his anger at circumstances controlled by Dame Fate spill over into his relations with Hoorka-kin. *Are you getting so old and stupid?* Yet he refused to let any of this show on his face. He let the hand holding the vibro fall to his side.

"You're both out of rotation until further notice," he

said. "You'll do apprentice work if that's all you're capable of. Aldhelm, do I need to see you work again?

"An elementary lesson, children. We're but one step removed from outlaw or lassari. No other world of the Alliance accepts us, and only this one backwater world allows us to work, due to its own code of bloodfeud. We're free *because* we have no loyalty to those in power—because the Neweden Assembly and the Alliance know that we follow our code. *My* code. We have no alliances: we can be trusted to side with no person or no cause. We're social carnivores feeding on death without caring what beast provides the meal. Do you see what the Li-Gallant will be thinking? We allowed Gunnar to escape because we've allied ourselves with him—that's his thought, if I know the man at all. To his mind, we've lost our adherence to the code. Bunglers!"

The Thane shoved the vibro back into its scabbard. The leather, blackened with age, showed much use. "Wipe your face, Aldhelm. I should have you both cast from the kin for last night. It's good that I know you both and have respect for your earlier work—and because I love you as guild-kin. It appeases my anger." Then his voice softened, though his dark eyes didn't.

"I know: because of my code, the victim has a chance of survival. I just wish it hadn't been *this* one. I wish She of the Five had looked a little more kindly on the Hoorka."

Aldhelm daubed at the blood on his cheek with the sleeve of his night-cloak while Sartas glanced quickly from his companion to the Thane.

"I've never seen Her so much against us. Gunnar could have stood against the entire kin." Aldhelm looked at the blood on his cloak, then at the Thane. "But I'll accept the blame for this, Thane. My dagger missed its target, and it shouldn't."

The Thane glanced at him, immersed in hidden guilt. Yah, he thought, it's not the fault of these two; it was Dame Fate's doing. But it's easier to chastise men than gods, and the anger/fear demanded release. He stroked his beard as the lamps coaxed red highlights from the graying hair. "Extra knife work for the two of you," he said finally. "At least you followed the dawn code. The Alliance might have had someone observing. I'll try to redeem our standing with the Li-Gallant, if I can. Go on, you must both be hungry and tired after a night's fruitless chasing. Get something from the kitchens, though neither of you deserve it."

The two Hoorka turned. As they were about to walk away, the Thane called to Aldhelm, prodded by his conscience. Aldhelm swiveled on his toes and looked back, his cerulean eyes cold.

"I didn't mean to cut you, Aldhelm. No one should draw the blood of kin, neh? I was angry, and I'm sorry for that."

Aldhelm shrugged. "I can understand your anger." Then, after a pause, "Thane." He nodded his head in leave.

"Truly, Aldhelm. My hand . . ." The Thane grappled briefly with the truth. ". . . slipped."

Aldhelm's eyebrows raised slightly. "I said I understand," he said, his voice flat.

"Rest well, then."

The two Hoorka walked away, the compacted earth under their feet making a gritty rasp. The memory of Aldhelm's chilly eyes remained with the Thane for a long time as he watched the nightcloaks blend with the darkness. *Was I that far out of control of myself?* He slammed a fist into his open hand.

"That won't do much good. It only makes your hand sore."

The Thane started and turned quickly, then straightened with a slight smile. The lines on his scarred face deepened. "Cranmer. I'd forgotten you were here."

"I'd wager you forgot more than that." Cranmer, a short, slight man by Neweden standards, indicated the passage down which Aldhelm and Sartas had gone. "I've never seen you that way, Thane. I don't think you intended to be so, ahh, cruel." Cranmer chose his words carefully, but censure rode lightly on the surface. An elfin figure in the twilight of the caverns, the small man blew on his cupped hands, holding them out above the thermal duct. "You almost warmed the cavern with your anger."

The Thane didn't reply. He took the tether of the hoverlamps and put them on the clips of his belt, slaving the lamps to him. Quickly-shifting wedges of light pursued themselves over the lines of his body, sending distorted shadows to fighting on the creviced walls and ceiling of the cavern. Cranmer, grunting, rose from his seat on the floater and absently wiped at his pants before throwing his cloak around him, muffling himself to the chin. Underasgard stayed a constant but cool temperature in the regions where the Hoorka did not live, and even here it was comfortable for most Neweden natives. But Cranmer always felt chilled, used as he was to a more temperate offworld climate.

The Thane completed his gathering of hoverlamps. The brilliant globes arrayed themselves about him like attendant suns around a god. Held in the stressed magnetic fields of the tethers, they bobbed slightly, never quite at rest, giving everything they illuminated a shivering animation. In this shifting atmosphere, the Thane watched Cranmer pick up his recorder and walk toward him over the broken rock of the cave floor.

"You were making a record of all that? I'm not sure I'm pleased."

"It seemed rather important to the sociological aspects of Hoorka, and you did give me leave to record as I wished." Cranmer eyed the Thane, looking for irritation in that well-used face. The confrontation with Aldhelm and Sartas had shown him a new aspect of that personality he'd thought he knew so well. Still, he failed to detect anything but simple curiosity in the Thane's question.

"It looked as if it might have some bearing on my study of Hoorka," he continued. "The image won't be too good. The lamps are really too dim for this unit. It'll be rather grainy." The cloak around him moved and rippled as he put the recorder in a pocket.

The Thane made a noise that might have been affirmation. He looked about, waiting, as Cranmer sealed out any possible draft in his cloak.

"Would you care to see some of the inner sections of the caverns?" The Thane nodded his head to the gathered darkness to his right, and for the first time Cranmer saw a cleft between the rocks. He sighed, relinquishing the thought of his comfortable heater back in the Hoorka caverns. But it wasn't often that the Thane offered tours.

"If you're willing. I've never gone further than this room."

The Thane nodded, knowing that the little man sensed that it wasn't simple courtesy that had moved the Thane to make this offer. He gave Cranmer two of the tethers and watched while the man strapped them to his waist, over his cloak.

"A Hoorka would put the tethers *under* the cloak. It won't affect the holding field, and the cloak, as you have it, will bind your movements."

Cranmer shook his head. Two shadow heads moved in sympathy. "It's warmer this way, and I'm not planning to do any fighting. Why else have a Hoorka with you, if not to do your fighting! And I'm *cold*." He shivered, involuntarily.

The Thane laughed, and echoes rose to share his amusement. "Scholars."

"Fighters," Cranmer replied, and smiled back at him, glad that the Thane seemed to have recovered some of his humor. He nodded toward the passage. "You're the guide, then. Lead."

They began walking, satin night retreating before them, giving way softly and grudgingly and falling back into place behind them. The Underasgard caverns, a system not yet completely mapped, were judged to be among the largest cave systems in the Alliance. The Thane made his way easily through the tumbled rocks with the nonchalance of one who had been this way before. The smaller and less muscular Cranmer followed with more difficulty—unlike the inhabited sections of the Hoorka caverns, the floor here hadn't been cleared of rubble and ionized to a dustless, flat perfection. Cranmer picked his way slowly over the slippery rock. The dull clunking of stone against stone marked their progress. Milky-white clusters of mineral crystals splotched the gray-blue walls, a stone fungus. The narrow passageway opened out into a large room that the lamps failed to light fully, then narrowed again until the Thane was forced to stoop to avoid striking his head on the roof—Cranmer could walk upright. They slid over a scree of small pebbles and around a fractured slab of roofstone. Another room opened up before them, the lamps only dimly showing its perimeters. There the Thane stopped and pointed to a large recess under a projecting shelf of rock.

"I found this quite some time ago, but I've yet to show it to Hoorka-kin. I've questioned my reluctance to point it out, but I haven't any answers." The Thane laughed, more a modulated exhalation than amusement. "Count yourself privileged, neh?" He fumbled with a tether holder, turning the field off and holding the lamp globe in his hand. He opened the shutters wide and threw the ball toward the darkness of the shelf. The lamp bounced and rolled, wild shadows darting crazily. When it settled, they could see the white arch of an ippicator skeleton, the rib cage upright, the two left legs and three right ones sprawled out to either side, while the small neck and head had fallen and lay in disorder.

"It's huge." Cranmer's voice was but a whisper.

"The largest I've seen," said the Thane, pride in his voice. He left unspoken the obvious value of the skeleton. Ippicators were an extinct Neweden animal, and the only assymetrical mammal yet discovered. Why they had developed the uneven arrangement of limbs was a question of great interest to palaeontologists, but what mattered to Neweden was that the skeletons were rare and their bones could be polished to a dull sheen—ippicator jewelery commanded a great price on the trade markets. This particular skeleton was, due to its size and condition, a thing of great potential wealth. The Thane, for his part, was determined that it would lie undisturbed.

Cranmer's stance and awed demeanor showed the impression the ippicator had made on him. The Thane smiled with pleasure. "I had it dated once: took a chip of bone and sent it to the Alliance labs in the Center. It's at least thirty thousand standards old. That makes it among the oldest ippicators found. And it's well-preserved. Those bones would hold a polish unlike any other."

The Thane settled himself on a rock and cupped his chin on his hands, staring at the skeleton. Cranmer fumbled in his cloak for his recorder, then hesitated. "You mind?" he asked.

The Thane shrugged. "As you like." He paused. "I like to imagine that beast, the most powerful of its kind

—perhaps an object of awe among its fellows—realizing that his time has come and that he's no longer capable of ruling the ippicator world. So the beast dragged himself in here, through that passage"—the Thane pointed to a darkness on the far side of the room—"and lay down. It was better than simply growing older and weaker until some stronger challenger fought him and won. A good way to end things, still in control."

"Too melodramatic. More likely it wandered in here and the stupid beast couldn't find its way back out." Cranmer pursed his lips. "Not that *I* could make my way back to the Hoorka caverns alone. So this is your meditation spot, yah?"

"I suppose that's as good a description as possible."

"It bothers you that the Hoorka-thane can have doubts, like the rest of common humanity? My friend, you're one of a small group of violent people on a violent world, interesting only in that you've set up an organization with a moralistic rationale that passes for philosophy, and a religious understructure that is, at best, loosely bound. It's hardly a thing to make the Alliance rise or fall. You worry overmuch."

"And Sondall-Cadhurst Cranmer speaks strongly for a scholar here by the grace of the one he insults, and he has the arrogance of most Alliance people I've met." The Thane used the impersonal mode of insult, the one most likely to cause offense on Neweden, and the one least likely to affect Cranmer. He smiled, with a tint of self-effacing sadness. "I'm not angry, Cranmer. I understand what you're saying, but this small world is the one on which I've built Hoorka, and Hoorka—what it does and where it goes—is of primary importance to me. Like the rest of the kin, I've given it my primary allegiance. This is my family, and I owe it my loyalty. Hoorka owns me, not the Alliance."

"Are you having doubts as to your ability to deal with the problems of Hoorka?"

"I didn't say that." The Thane's voice was sharp in the quiet of the cavern.

"I apologize, then. I thought you might be hinting . . . ah, never mind." Cranmer pitched a small stone into the darkness. Together they listened to it rattle and stop. The echoes eddied, growing steadily weaker until they died. There was a long silence, then, as both men stared at the skeleton.

"I don't know my own mind any more," the Thane said, finally. He rubbed a muscular thigh with his hand, then stretched his legs out in front of him. "I'm not growing any younger, certainly, and the Hoorka problems are becoming more complicated as we grow. I hope the code can hold us together, that Dame Fate lets us survive. I know we'll survive, if Hoorka-kin will let themselves be governed by the code."

"Then you're not thinking of finding some back cavern and crawling in to die?" Cranmer made a show of switching off his recorder and putting it back in his pocket. "I'm disappointed."

The Thane smiled, adding to Cranmer's laugh. "Disappointed that I don't react as my ippicator? No, the analogy's a poor one, anyway. Didn't you tell me that from all indications, the ippicator was most likely a herbivore? That doesn't sound like Hoorka-kin."

Cranmer snorted in derision. "Thane, I'm an archeo-sociologist, not a digger into dead bones. But yes, I seem to recall that in one of my university classes back on Niffleheim, I was told that the ippicator was a lowly grass-eater. I think so, at least."

The Thane waved his hand. "It doesn't matter."

Velvet silence settled in on them again, pressing down like a tangible substance. The Thane could hear Cranmer breathing and the whisper of cloth against flesh as he moved. When Cranmer spoke, the sound startled him with its loudness.

"Thane, what happened back there with Aldhelm and Sartas? I've never seen you succumb to your anger before. The Hoorka *must* fail to kill their victims at times—it's part of your code; Dame Fate has to have Her chance. Yes, it was the Li-Gallant's contract, but surely he'll understand what happened—and since the contract was unsuccessful, you won't be revealing who signed the contract. He's safe from retribution. Why were you so upset?"

"So I have to explain again?" The Thane swept to his feet. The hoverlamps followed him, and light flickered madly about the cavern. The bones of the ippicator danced in the moving light. "It's *Vingi's* contract," the Thane said, his voice oddly quiet, "not some guild-feud jealousy or a personal feud. The Li-Gallant's contract. I don't want his paranoia affecting Hoorka. The Alliance has been watching us closely, even to the extent of giving us a contract in their sector of Sterka Port—and the Alliance is more important than Neweden, if I ever want Hoorka to go offworld. But Neweden—and Vingi—can foul that dream. That's the importance."

"Because you're afraid that this organization you've built has a faulty structure and can't survive a few questionings? Your protestations are surface, Thane. Something else had to drive you to lash out at your own kin when you knew they were blameless." Cranmer's voice was soft and he looked not at the Thane, but at the ippicator.

"*Damn* you, Cranmer!" The Thane's voice was suddenly hoarse with venom. Cranmer turned at the shout and saw the Thane's hand on the hilt of his vibro.

And as suddenly as it had flared, the anger drained away and his hand moved to his side, away from his weapon, though his eyes were still held in sharp lines of flesh. *He's right, old man. He's right, and that's why you're angry. Because he's pricked the core of your uncertainty. Because you always considered your emotions too well-hidden to be fathomed. Fool.* "You've had time to study Hoorka, scholar." He stressed the last word slightly too much. "What do you think?"

"*I* don't know. But I never get angry at my ignorance."

"Some things are too large to be angry with." The Thane watched Cranmer slowly relax as the smaller man realized that the irritation was gone from the Thane's voice. "I'm surprised you maintain your interest in us."

"I've been interested enough to have taken two extensions of my leave from Niffleheim Center."

The Thane shrugged. He watched Cranmer draw his cloak tighter around him, noting for the first time the man's growing discomfort from the cold of the room.

The Thane glanced a last time at the ippicator skeleton, shrugged again, and took a step toward the passage leading back to the Hoorka sector. "I'm tired of talk, and I've much to do back in Hoorka-home. If you've seen enough of our five-legged friend . . ."

"Thane, I'm willing to listen more, if that's what you need. The recorder's off, and I keep secrets."

"I wouldn't have shown you the ippicator if I hadn't been sure of your discretion." He shook his head and allowed his features to relax, his shoulders to sag. "No, I've tormented you with enough of my idiocy. But I thank you for the offer." A pause. "Friend."

Cranmer got to his feet. The Thane leading, they followed the sounds of their footsteps back to familiar ground.

Three

Vingi's keep huddled against the Port barrier, as if drawing comfort from its proximity to that demarcation line between Neweden and land that was officially Alliance territory. The keep was a massive building of local white stone. Turrets flowered unexpectedly from one side, while a row of thin caryatids masked the front facing the city. Like most Neweden estates, it had its gardens, though these were larger than most, with plants coaxed into geometric patterns around which the footpaths meandered. A brook threw foam as it made its way around the rocks lining its bed; ground birds preened in their iridescent plumage. As a symbol of Vingi's wealth and power, it was more than effective: a pretty but useless display. Vingi would starve were he reduced to eating the produce of his gardens. Still, it flaunted his success in the face of the poor world in which it stood.

The Thane, quite irrevocably, hated it.

The Hoorka felt the habitual disgust the keep grounds always engendered in him. Standing before the gates (real metal, not a shield: more ostentation and non-utility) he could see the great contrast between the keep and the rest of Sterka—and Sterka was the richest of Neweden's cities, thanks to the trade of the Port. The Thane, who had seen most of the other urban centers, knew that the Keep was far and away the most lavish display of wealth on Neweden, shadowing even the famous Temple of Khala built by the Guild of Artisans.

And like any Neweden native, he knew that the wealth of Vingi derived not from Vingi but from his kin-father, a brilliant but cruel ruler who had leeched money from kin and kinless without a thought and built a base of power none had assailed. Vingi—now Li-Gallant, as his kin-father had been before him—had inherited that man's cruelty but not his intelligence. It wasn't a pleasant combination.

But, the Thane mused as he showed his pass to the gate ward, Neweden seemed none the worse for it. Guilds still fought with guilds, and kinship of guilds mattered more than biological ancestry, and lassari were still poor and despised. Nothing had changed.

It took much time to breach the layers of officialdom that shielded Vingi from the common public. The Thane was handed from attendant to attendant; from the gate ward to a garden-steward to a bland receptionist who ushered him into a waiting room and left him to stare at undecorated walls for several minutes. Finally, a secretary opened the door and beckoned to the Thane to follow—by the badge on the woman's uniform, she'd been accepted into Vingi's ruling guild and was now due the full respect of a person with kin. He bowed to her politely and entered the Li-Gallant's office. The secretary bowed herself out.

The Li-Gallant was standing at a window, his back to the Thane. He said nothing in the way of salutation, but began speaking as if in the middle of a conversation.

"I failed to see a body at the gates this morning, Thane." Vingi continued looking at the garden. His ornate robes of office moved with his breathing.

The Thane, knowing it would irritate the Li-Gallant, seated himself in a floater near the desk that dominated the room. The Li-Gallant, hearing no answer to his statement, opaqued the window and turned to see the Thane already seated. He grimaced. Rings flared from his gold-banded and pudgy fingers. "I asked a question, Hoorka. I have kin, and I'll brook no insult from anyone. Speak, man."

The Thane didn't move, nor did his eyes flinch. He spoke with distillate calm. "There was no body to give you, Li-Gallant. Gunnar survived. He lived until our dawn. I can't put it any more simply for you, nor do I think I owe you any further explanation." A moment. "With all respect due kin, Li-Gallant."

Vingi backed away from the assassin, his face screaming undisguised anger, though his body sought to put the comforting bulwark of his desk between himself and the Hoorka. The Thane's lassitude increased Vingi's nervousness, made his bladder ache to be emptied.

"You followed my orders?" The Li-Gallant seated himself.

"We followed the code. You've read the contract, Li-Gallant. The victim is given his chance. We're not murderers, not acting for our own kin in bloodfeud. We tilt the scales of life and death, but we don't presume to be gods, able to take life at whim. That is Her perogative." The Thane bowed his head at the mention of She of the Five and watched Vingi expel an irritated breath. Good, he thought, Vingi's upset, and our failure is justified ethically. Let him try to bring us before the Assembly. For the first time, he had hopes of leaving the keep with Hoorka safe.

"I've no interest in the gods of your kin," the Li-Gallant said, "simply in results."

"Results are often in a god's control."

Vingi scowled. "What weapons did your people use?"

"Daggers from Khaelia. The Alliance brought them to us as payment for a contract a few months ago. Very effective."

"Obviously." Vingi waited for a reaction to his sarcasm and received none. He hurried to fill the silence. "Why didn't you use firearms? Lasers?"

"Li-Gallant, Gunnar had no bodyshield. The odds would have been over-balanced, and Dame Fate would have been angered. It isn't our intention to tamper with destinies. If a person dies by the Hoorka, then he wasn't meant for survival. If he lives, he was meant to live. The weak: they fall. The strong—perhaps they live. If that's cruel, it's no crueler than Dame Fate Herself." The Thane folded his hands on the gray-black cloth of his lap as his eyes glittered darkly, daring objection. He sounded bored, as if reciting a lesson to a child.

"I should have sent my own people." Vingi's right hand made a bejeweled fist that hovered indecisively over the marbled desk top. The fist was an impotent weapon, speaking of too much disuse to be a symbol of anything but wealth. The Thane's lips curled in a vestige of a smile that flickered for an instant and was gone.

"You sent your forces," he said. "They interfered with the two assassins and were in part to blame for Gunnar's escape. I wouldn't bring that up before the Assembly, Li-Gallant, but let's not try to deceive ourselves here. You sent four killers of your own—and without declaring bloodfeud, which the Neweden Assembly might find interesting—and they failed. Accuse Hoorka, Li-Gallant, and Hoorka will speak the truth. Again, with no disrespect."

Vingi didn't deny the veracity of the Thane's words. The raised fist struck the desk with soft anger. Papers scattered there didn't move.

"Almost," he said.

"They killed Ricia Cuscratti, Gunnar's mistress, I believe." The Hoorka's voice seemed devoid of any emotion, but behind the words was contempt. "I understand that, as kin-lord of a competing guild, you've sent a tithing to defray the expense of the death rites. A gift. I hope it eased your conscience."

"M'Dame Cuscratti's death was unfortunate but almost unavoidable. She was harboring Gunnar." Vingi smiled. "And *if* those people responsible are ever found, my government will punish them. They'll pay the fine for accidental death."

"Ahh." *So he won't admit it, even privately.*

"I fail to see, in any event, what bearing that has on the failure of Hoorka."

"It caused the two Hoorka trailing Gunnar to lose several hours. Had, ahh, the person who sent the intruders more trust in the Hoorka, *you* might have had your death."

"I'm not interested in excuses."

"We've no need for excuses. The Hoorka had to deal with interference. It doesn't matter who caused it. But I intend to post notice of feud with the Assembly, should we find those responsible. So I wish your investigation success, neh?" The Thane waved a disparaging hand. "The Hoorka can also play the game of pretended ignorance."

Vingi shrugged. The cloth of his robes glistened with

interwoven metallic strands. The Thane allowed himself another brief moment of amusement. Vingi compounded distrust on distrust. That fabric would turn back the sting of any hand weapon, and the Thane was certain that when he'd arrived he'd been surreptitiously searched: beamed and probed. He also knew that if he intended to kill the obese man before him, he wouldn't need any weapon other than his hands. The Li-Gallant didn't trust him—that was obvious, and it was disturbing. The Hoorka-guild was based on the precept that no Hoorka would kill unless threatened or contracted to do so. Never without warning, unlike the other guilds, who declared bloodfeud at the slightest provocation. Vingi's uncertainty in the face of that code was a bad omen.

The Thane decided to waste no more time. "You have our payment, I suppose?"

Vingi's face became a rictus, a snarl. "You demand a large price for small results."

"You know the code, and you declined to pay in advance." There was no apology in the Thane's voice. It lashed at the Li-Gallant with feigned nonchalance. Yet the Thane knew that this was a dangerous moment. He felt uncertainty in his tactics. *Do I doubt myself so much? Where is the vaunted confidence?*

"I've registered a complaint with the Neweden Assembly." There was a triumphant sneer on Vingi's face, a vestige of bravado. "The Alliance Regent, m'Dame d'Embry, has expressed her interest in this situation, and I felt it might aid her, as she has said that she would like answers to the questions I've raised."

"You play dangerously, Li-Gallant, if I may speak frankly. I wouldn't care to have a bloodfeud between your kin and mine, were I you. We are trained for fighting."

"You'll be notified when to appear, Thane. You must admit that circumstances—despite any protestations of interference from, ahh, outside sources—are suspicious. If the Hoorka are aligned with Gunnar's party, they're a danger to the stability of Neweden government. Surely you see that. No disrespect intended for Hoorka. I merely wish to have an account of that night."

"Do you intend to reveal that you signed the contract?"

The Li-Gallant laughed. "I'm not so foolish, Thane. And should it happen that Gunnar learns that I was the signer, it would simply add to the suspicions."

"It still wouldn't be wise or prudent to neglect our payment, Li-Gallant." The Thane stood abruptly, his night-cloak swirling. Vingi started, his eyes wide, and his hands disappeared below the surface of the desk. The Thane could see him fumbling for something unseen there.

"Should I think you were summoning your guards, Li-Gallant, I might take it as a personal affront. I could easily appease my wounded dignity before they could enter." The Thane hoped he'd taken the right path, had gauged Vingi's fear correctly. If not—he thrust the apprehensions from him.

"I don't care for your threats, Hoorka," Vingi replied, but his hands were now still. "If we were in public . . ."

The Thane said nothing, waiting. In the silence, the sound of a muffled voice could be heard in Vingi's outer office, followed by a high, clear laugh. It held no threat.

The Li-Gallant brought his hands up and slid a pastel check across his desk. The Hoorka-thane smiled, his eyes openly laughing, and he leaned forward to take the payment.

"Our thanks, Li-Gallant."

The Thane walked easily through the streets: easily because the throngs parted before him with an apprehensive glance at the black and gray nightcloak of the Assassin's Guild. Gray and black: no colors, no loyalty except to Hoorka-kin. The aura of the deathgods hung about him, subtle and menacing, and none cared to taint themselves by approaching too closely to this impassive man. They were used to hardship and death—the people of Neweden, a ghetto world by any standard—but the Hoorka were hardened and deadly beyond the norm. Better they be avoided. That was the consensus.

The check from the Li-Gallant didn't give the Thane as much pleasure as he'd expected. He had anticipated Vingi's covert avoidance of payment, the hedging of an angered ruler. But Vingi's anger had been something beyond the measured and calculating displeasure of a kin's defense of offended pride, and it wasn't in the Li-Gallant's nature to let his ire fester long within himself. He'd exorcize the demon. How, and how would it affect Hoorka? The question nagged at him. Surely Vingi wouldn't be so foolish as to declare this a matter of bloodfeud between their guilds? Vingi's kin would die, and that would allow Gunnar's ruling guild access to vacant seats on the Assembly. No, something more devious.

The populace noised about him as the Thane passed through a market square. Carts loaded with produce were surrounded by shouting buyers while farmers bellowed vaguely-heard prices and boasted of the quality of their particular products. Someone brushed against the Thane's side and muttered a quick, overly-sincere apology as he darted back into the crowd. Here and there a few flashily-clothed Diplos—members of the Alliance Diplomatic Resources Team—made their way through the milling people, but even they, the aristocracy protected by the offworld power of the Alliance, gave the Thane wide berth. It was, after all, a Neweden jest that even the Dead would part to let a Hoorka pass.

The Thane walked slowly, letting the noise and bustle fade to the edges of his conciousness, thinking—

—the Li-Gallant wants Gunnar dead, and he wants to know whether the Hoorka have sided with his opposition. He'll find a way to determine if his paranoia is founded in truth or not. But how will he go about it, what can he do?

—and what bothers me? Once I would have reveled in a confrontation like this, would have enjoyed the knife-edge of tension. Now I'm simply tired and unsure—I'd avoid this if I could. Cranmer's thought: is it time to step aside? Should Aldhelm or Mondom or someone else be Thane? No. No.

—it's a fine day. The sunstar shines, She of the Five smiles. But my frown puzzles these people. Do they think I'm contemplating my next contract, that I'm daydreaming of spilled blood and death? And how many of them, thinking my imagined thoughts distasteful, would still advise their kin to come to Hoorka to settle a bloodfeud with another guild?

—I should rest. I've been so tired lately. Perhaps

Mondom—but no, that relationship has passed. Too many complications—

He touched the pouch in which the check rode and smiled, forcibly evicting his pessimism. Passersby shook their heads at the evil omen.

The Hoorka smile only at death.

The Thane was nearly across the market square, in the bluish shadow cast by the spires of the Tri-Guild Church. Just ahead of him, a man shoved his way through the throngs before the Hoorka. The Hoorka could see the wake of the disturbance spreading as people scattered, and in a brief clear space he caught a brief glimpse of the problem. A man without a badge of kinship—a lassari, kin-less and status-less—was shoving aside those in front of him. Then the crowds closed in again, pushing. The Thane saw a blur of blue-and-yellow-tinted flesh as a woman was knocked to the pavement, though he couldn't tell if it were due to the manic lassari or the pressure of the crowd. He started to walk away at an angle to the welling struggling as a roar of wordless protest began to rise. He kept a scowl on his face, relying on that and the uniform of the Hoorka to make his way.

"Hoorka! I see you!" The shout came as the lassari thrust aside those nearest the Thane and entered the clear space about the Hoorka. The Thane continued walking, ignoring the man—he had a brief impression of frantic, dark eyes and a thin, wiry body clothed in dingy wraps—but the shout was repeated, imperious and commanding.

"Hoorka!"

The Thane halted and turned slowly. From the corner of his eyes he saw the crowd in the square moving to a safe distance from the confrontation, forming a rough circle about the two. The man was armed: the Thane could see the wavering orange fleck of a vibro tip in the man's right hand, and the Hoorka swept his nightcloak over his shoulder, out of the way of his arms.

"A problem, sirrah?" The honorific was a mockery in his voice. Lassari were not due the respect of those with kin, and his intonation made it clear that he was mocking the man. It was, however, a truism that an angered lassari made a dangerous enemy—they didn't have the worry of the safety of their fellow guild members. The Thane kept his eyes on the vibro arm, wary.

The lassari was breathing heavily, as if nervous or excited, and he shifted his weight from one foot to the other in a constant motion. The watching crowd moved a step further back.

"Hoorka!" the man shouted a third time. "You've destroyed me. I might as well mumble chants with the Dead. No one talks to me, no one deals with me. Lassari, they say, and spit. Your fault." The words were slurred, and from the distance of two meters, the Thane could smell the spicy odor of lujisa. The man was an addict, then, and a thief, for only a rich man or a thief could afford the offworld drug. On Neweden, there were no rich lassari. It also meant that he was beyond reason, lost in the false logic of an interior world with few touchstones to the reality around him. Lujisa addicts had been known to attack strangers because of a sudden whim or fancy. Was this such an accidental encounter? the Thane wondered. Then: could Vingi have arranged this so quickly after our meeting?

The Thane stalled, saying anything that came to mind as he studied the man. "I don't know you. Hoorka-kin doesn't know you. You've mistaken me for another, perhaps? I have nothing to do with you, and I don't see you, lassari." He spoke tentatively, watching for any reactions his words had on the man.

"You DO!" The last word was a scream that echoed from the spires of the church. Birds took quick flight from the rooftops and settled down again slowly. The lassari spat on the pavement and shook his head as if annoyed by some insect. "The Hoorka wouldn't accept me as apprentice. You made me lassari." He scuffed at the ground. "You did it. You know me."

"I don't even see you. And Hoorka chooses its kin as it pleases." He waited, then spoke again. "I don't see you. You don't exist to me, lassari."

There seemed to be nothing else to do. The insult came grudgingly from his lips. The susurrus from the watching crowd held them, as aware as the Thane that there was nothing else he could do. The attack would come, or not:

who could tell? Lujisa made for strange behavior, and until the lassari moved, he was trapped. The Thane moved his hand fractionally closer to his vibro.

And as if that action had triggered a reflex in the lassari, the man lunged without warning. The Thane, more out of instinct than intent, stepped back and to one side, his hands reaching for the attacker. The hum of the vibro dopplered past his ear, and the Thane chopped at the man as his momentum carried the lassari past the Hoorka. The lassari twisted in an effort to stop his fall and the Thane's blow caught him on the shoulder. The Thane pivoted to see the man roll and gain his feet—the crowd retreating frantically as the lassari came near them. The Thane watched the hand holding the vibro and the waist: his training—the training he'd in turn imparted to Hoorka-kin—had taught him that while a person may feint with any part of his body, the hips must go in the direction of movement. The Thane unsheathed and activated his vibro as the lassari regained his footing.

The man's next charge was unsubtle, lacking any pretense or grace. With a flick of his wrist, the Thane brought his nightcloak over the man's vibro arm as he cut at him with his own weapon. The lassari screamed in pain as the vibro tip gashed his side. He went limp, dropping his weapon. The Thane kicked it away as the man rolled on the ground, clutching his wounded side. The crowd moved in closer, drawn to the agony.

The Thane shut off his vibro and sheathed it. He was breathing heavily, tired far beyond the little effort he'd needed. He looked down at the moaning lassari. "I had no quarrel with you, no-kin-of-mine. And Hoorka do not kill unless paid to do so. Not even lassari." He let his cloak fall back around him, and the people moved to give him a corridor through the crowd. Trying not to show his weariness, the Thane walked away, his face forbidding comment.

As he passed from the square into the narrow back streets of Sterka, he found all the vague pleasure of the day gone. It was unusual enough for a Hoorka to be attacked, but this confrontation nagged at him with implications beyond the surface. Had Vingi, or even Gunnar, arranged it, as a way of avoiding a declaration of formal bloodfeud with the Hoorka? Had it been intentional and not simply an accident of timing and circumstance—a whim of Dame Fate?

Lastly—and it bothered the Thane that this seemed important—could he have avoided the fight, could he have eased himself away without knifing the man?

After all, what insult was there to the deranged maunderings of a lassari and lujisa addict?

The questions pounded at him, one with the throbbing in his chest and the troubling wheeze he could hear in his lungs.

He moved in his clear space through the streets. The sunstar sparked lazy motes of dust in the air. Birds foraged for crumbs in the central gutter of the street.

The Thane walked toward the city gates.

Four

"At the core of the Hoorka philosophy, if that's what this, ahh, moral code with religion must be called, is a shrewd knowledge of Neweden mores and cultural patterns. The Hoorka exist through the practice of guild-kinship —Neweden's replacement for the biological, nuclear family —*and* the normal jealousies to which humans are prone. Now; no, make that: Since the advent of the Hoorka, there is an alternative offered Neweden. Rather than calling a formal bloodfeud between guilds and the possibility of carnage that that entails and by all the gods, that's a clumsy sentence. Umm, cancel and begin program, please.

"The Hoorka function as an alternative to the traditional method of settling conflicts: the bloodfeud. On Neweden, a bloodfeud may become a small-scale war, all perfectly legal. By contacting the Hoorka and signing their contract, a person can fulfill his duty to his kin or his gods for any insult, and still retain his life with his pride.

"The Hoorka price is high, but that fits in with their crude; no, make that"—(pause)—"*unsophisticated* variation on Social Darwinism: in essence, crude survival of the fit. They contend that wealth is an outgrowth of power and fitness—and yet the victim retains a chance of escaping this harsh justice, for the victim may have 'survival traits' that are not tied in with the accumulation of lucre. The odds are never overloaded in the favor of the Hoorka. If the victim isn't carrying a bodyshield, as an example, the Hoorka will decline to carry firearms or stings in carrying out the contract. This aspect of the code has had a corollary effect: most contracted victims decline to use such technologically-based defenses, relying instead upon speed and stealth."

Cranmer reached over the desk to switch off the voicetyper and then looked at the words he'd just written. "Anything particularly wrong with that, Thane? It's simply for my notes. What eventually gets put together for publication will be scattered with a more esoteric vocabulary so that the University people don't feel their intelligence is being insulted—if they can understand a concept too easily, they think it below their notice."

"You sound mildly bitter, scholar."

Cranmer leaned back in his floater and put his hands behind his head. He pursed his lips, eyes closed. "No, just realistic. I've been away from it long enough to have an objectivity about the drawbacks of my profession. I don't care for that much posturing and pretension in anyone but myself." He grinned. "And *that's* a normal human instinct."

The Thane had been standing near the shield that cut this—Cranmer's rooms—from the other caverns of Underasgard. Now he moved forward and sat on the bed. Above him, a lamp tinted gold threw light down on the crown of the Thane's head, so that every line of his face was accentuated. The Thane caught sight of himself in a mirror across the room, and he grimaced. He moved slightly, so that the light struck him at an angle, softening his face. He surreptitiously examined the results, hoping Cranmer hadn't noticed his vanity. "Wait until we Hoorka go offworld. You'll have to revise your paper."

Cranmer frowned. He leaned forward toward the Thane, his eyes questioning. "Thane, in the months I've spent with you, I've never hedged truths. If the Hoorka *do* go offworld—and I don't know that d'Embry's ever going to allow that—I think you're going to run into far more trouble remaining consistent than you realize. You'll be operating under totally different social structures, if nothing else. The code might have to be re-worked to some degree. You're set up for Neweden, not Nifflheim or Longago or Aris. This planet is the only one of which I'm aware that has such a hidebound caste system—the guilds—and *they* are what make the Hoorka code work."

"The code is sufficient." The Thane shook his head in disagreement. Light shifted across his face. "If we start tampering with our structure, making exceptions and addendums here and there, what will distinguish us from common criminals? No," he said emphatically, "I've thought of this before. I don't see where the structure of any other society will be so alien that the code would fail."

"I'm not suggesting that the code become fluid."

"That's good. Then perhaps you do understand Hoorka."

"Do the two of you do nothing but argue all day?" Both men turned to the doorshield to see Mondom standing there, a gentle smile on her face, her hands on her hips in mock disgust. Short dark hair frothed the side of her thin, finely-featured face and neck. A nightcloak was clasped around her shoulders, masking her figure.

"Come in, m'Dame," the Thane said. She nodded. Her lithe, athletic body moved with a grace that the Thane remembered with pleasure and envy. She sat on the foot of the bed, near the Thane.

Cranmer had sat back in his floater again, half-reclining, his head staring at the ceiling. "I was informing our revered Thane that sometimes the creation has to transcend the creator—my old line, I realize—but all things are subject to modification, if they want to survive."

Mondom laughed, a crystalline sound. "Not a philosophy that would appeal to him, neh?" She placed a cool hand briefly over the Thane's, then withdrew it. The Thane glanced at her; she smiled in return.

"Or to most Hoorka, I would hope." The Thane chuckled to show that he was jesting, but he was remembering Mondom's hand. "Cranmer's simply caught up in a vision of the perfect thesis, neatly bound and impervious to logic."

"And life *isn't* definable in terms of a thesis, then? Gods, my colleagues will be profoundly disappointed to hear that. They'll mull it over for a year and then write a paper on it. Smash their entire concept of reality . . ." He thumped the voicetyper for emphasis. The three of them laughed. Cranmer looked from Mondom to the Thane. He shoved the floater back from his desk and stretched his arms out, fingers interlocked. Joints cracked aridly, and Mondom winced.

"I guess I should wander off and see who's on kitchen duty," Cranmer said. "Thinking's hard enough work for us sedentary types—and from the look on m'Dame Mondom's face, she has business to discuss. Yah?"

Mondom nodded, smiling. "And you should take some exercise. That's a flabby body you carry with you."

"Would I then stand a chance with you, m'Dame?" Cranmer struck a melodramatically romantic pose.

"Possibly, sirrah." Over-coyly.

"I'll see the two of you later, then." Cranmer, whistling a motet off-key, waved a hand at the two Hoorka as he left the room. Mondom watched the doorshield close again behind him and turned to the Thane.

"I'll miss the little man when he leaves us," she said.

The Thane, looking at the papers neatly stacked beside the typer, nodded his head in agreement. "As will I. I need his objectivity, however galling it sometimes becomes."

"Well, he was right; I do have business to discuss with you." Mondom pulled a flimsy from the breast pocket of her nightcloak. Paper crackled as she unfolded it. "You said to notify you when the next contract arrived. I just received one." She glanced at the document. "From a Jast Claswell of the Bard's Guild, to attempt the killing of an E. J. Dausset, of the Engineers."

The Thane sighed as he moved, stretching out a hand to take the flimsy from Mondom. He moved so that the light from the hoverlamp fell full on the paper, putting him in shadow. "I know I'm due next in the rotation. Who was I to be teamed with?"

"D'Mannberg."

The Thane nodded and handed the contract back to Mondom. As her eyes watched him, he walked a few steps toward the wall. He rested his hand on the cool rock, then turned back to her. "Move him back in the rotation and have Aldhelm posted to go with me." He wiped his hand, damp from the chill of the rock, absently on his cloak. He looked up to see surprise raise Mondom's eyebrows, but she lowered her gaze at first contact and folded the flimsy slowly and deliberately. When she did speak, her voice and manner were carefully devoid of question or censure; because of that, it was obvious to the Thane that she was disturbed.

"Am I to give Aldhelm an explanation?"

The Thane shook his head. "No, I just want to cause our kin to think of the Gunnar mistake."

"Thane"—and now her voice spoke with soft, gentle reproach—"are you sure that's what you want to do? It won't help Aldhelm's mood. You haven't seen him today. Your chastisement, his own guilt at having let Gunnar escape when he knew full well the importance of that contract, the knife-cut . . ."

"I didn't mean to cut him," the Thane interrupted. His voice was high and loud with hurried protest. *Calm, calm. Why do you allow yourself to become upset so quickly?*

"I know—and he knows, whether he cares to admit it or not." Mondom's voice soothed him. She'd always been able to do so, when they'd been lovers, and since then as a friend. "But that doesn't mean a great deal. He's not an apprentice or a new Hoorka. He's the best of the kin. What happened the other night was Dame Fate's whim, not Hoorka clumsiness. You didn't need to make an example of him."

Two spots of color flared high on the Thane's cheeks. "I have my own thoughts. I'm doing what I think is right, and I *do* rule the Hoorka. If you'd like to change that, call for a vote by the kin." *Haughty, so haughty.* He hated himself for the way the last sentence had sounded, but it was too late. *Why do you always hurt her?*

Mondom's hands described a helpless circle. She shook her head. "No, I can't agree with you. But I wouldn't say that anywhere but here, and if you insist, I'll go along with this." After a moment: "For what it's worth."

The Thane's expression softened as the ruddiness faded from his cheeks. He impulsively touched her hand, felt the callouses there, the broken fingernails.

"I appreciate that," he said. "I need the support, and Aldhelm would take the news better from you."

She shrugged, her eyes steady on his. She let her hand stay where it was. "I owe you that much."

Her forefinger stroked his palm and the Thane slowly let his hand fall back to his side. "That's all past. You owe me nothing."

"It's past only because you insist that it need to be so. I'd still sleep with you—and you haven't slept with any of the kin for some time. It needn't be me. A hint . . ." She smiled.

"You're too interested in other's affairs."

"They used to be partially mine, if you recall."

"And you know why I wanted to end it. It wasn't for my sake."

Mondom's smile faded. She rose from the bed and moved over to Cranmer's floater, and idly toyed with his 'typer, running her fingers over the controls. She switched on the machine, listened to its mechanical humming, then turned it off again. "I understand your intentions, Thane. I *don't* understand the reasoning. The code encourages a certain promiscuity among Hoorka-kin if they haven't formed a relationship with a single person—and it helps, with our imbalance of men to women. But you don't forbid monogamous relationships. You couldn't. You wouldn't want to. I remember your jealousy when I slept with Bronton. I even enjoyed it. You were so mutely gentle and hurt. You should be so open with your kin more often, love."

"I don't want it said that you're on the Hoorka Council because you are the Thane's bed partner."

Mondom flared with sudden anger. "I don't need your altruism *or* your protection. I can stand with my own abilities. I've told you that before. Let someone challenge me on the practice floor if they doubt my skills."

"This still makes it easier."

"For whom? You? Me?" Mondom spread her hands wide, the folds of the nightcloak shifting fluidly. "If you can't handle the relationship, tell me. That would be easier. But don't make excuses. I want truth, not evasions." Her voice was dangerously gentle. "Damn you, I still care for you—it doesn't matter if that's no longer mutual. It doesn't change the feelings. But tell me the truth, kin to kin."

"I don't know myself any more. Damn it, Mondom, we've had this argument before. It never does any good, and we go about for the next few days angry with ourselves because we've hurt one another. That's something I have no interest in doing." He paused, searching her eyes and drifting down to her set lips. "That's the truth."

"And I said I wouldn't bring it up again. I know." She pressed her lips together in a half-smile, a sad amusement. "I'm sorry. If you change your mind, you know where to find me. I'll go post the names for the Claswell contract. Aldhelm and yourself? You won't change that?"

"Neh. Aldhelm and myself." The Thane paused a moment, began to speak, then lapsed into silence.

"Go on." Mondom touched his hand, her forefinger moving from the wrist to the back of his veined hand and back again.

"It's nothing," he said, his eyes watching the slow caress of her finger. Then he looked up to see her watching. "I feel *old*, somehow, and I've never felt so uncertain before. And it's not age, but . . ." He shook his head. "I'm just tired of the intrigue, tired of the chase, the hunt. What was it Cranmer called us, an 'adolescent fantasy in a prepubescent world'? I'm weary of blood, and I keep looking for other solutions to our problems. And there don't seem to be any. Kin fight other kin, and kin always fight lassari, and Dame Fate laughs while Hag Death collects her due."

"You should hear yourself. Maudlin, love, maudlin."

"You should feel this way."

"Are you telling me you should step down as Thane?"

"*No*!" His denial was vigorous, and the vehemence startled even himself. "No," he repeated more gently. "Not yet, in any event. Post the names, would you?"

"As you wish." Mondom rose, then stepped toward the Thane. She stopped an arm's length from him and touched his face with her hand. She traced the line of his cheekbone, the furrow running from nostril to mouth. "I'm not angry. I just see you changing. You don't seem as confident in yourself as you once did, and I worry for you. For Hoorka, and for you. Because I still care."

Her hand dropped, and she walked quickly to the

doorshield, stepping through it before he could formulate a reply. The Thane sat on the bed for a long hour, steeping himself in frustration.

The domed roof of the Neweden Assembly Hall was set with stained-glass murals depicting the fall of Huard, works of art as famous for their beauty as for the difficulties involved in appeasing the seven major artisan's guilds. Each had wanted their guild commissioned for the work, and it was only through the determined efforts of the Assembly that the work had been done at all. Seven panes there were, and through each jeweled shafts of light fell in dusty pillars to the distant floor. Birds roosted in the gutters of the dome, spotting the murals with whitish droppings that were daily cleaned. Today, the birds' rest was disturbed by the faint sound of shouting voices below; bureaucratic strife and political dueling among the various guild-kin that composed the Assembly.

"The ruling guild of Sirrah Gunnar is at least concerned with the welfare of those people on Neweden that haven't the advantages of the Li-Gallant."

Potok leaned forward at his desk, shouting across the length of the Assembly Hall to the high dais where Vingi sat behind a bank of viewscreens. A stylus, held between forefinger and thumb, stabbed the air in Vingi's direction, and if Potok seemed a trifle more theatrical than was his wont—as a trio of holocameras recorded the scene with cyclopian indifference, broadcasting the meeting to the Diplo Center a few blocks away—nobody remarked upon it. Assembly meetings were half-stage production, half-serious at best, and much was tolerated that would, in the streets, be cause for declaration of bloodfeud.

The session thus far had proved to be one of the more entertaining for those in a position to find the semi-functioning of their Assembly amusing—which were those few who didn't depend on it in some way for the stability of their lives. Neweden's government—by law a republic with an elected head, the Li-Gallant—was in practice an economic dictatorship with Vingi as ruler through his holding of the monetary reins of the planet, a ruler as his kin-father had been before him. It was not always an efficient system, but like all governments it worked occasionally.

There was a shout from the far side of the floor, another of the many guild representatives. "Haven't we heard enough rhetoric designed simply to slow down the functioning of this Assembly? Li-Gallant, I respectfully ask that Representative Potok—"

Potok shouted down the man—he had good lungs. "*And I have the floor*, honored representative. If you'll be so good as not to interrupt me, this body may well function more efficiently." He turned, slowly and with exaggerated pride, to face Vingi again. The sunlight from above sparked and flared over the glittering satin of his ceremonial robes: turquoise, the color of his guild, Gunnar's guild. What he had just said, uttered in public, would have caused the other party to demand satisfaction. But candor, and what might be rudeness in normal Neweden society, were tolerated here. Potok glared at the Li-Gallant and pressed his point.

"I ask again, Li-Gallant, for an investigation into the attempted murder of our party leader. You've evaded giving a direct answer or letting the matter come to a vote. I request that you speak your mind and enlighten us down on the floor as to your reasoning."

Vingi squinted into the bluish haze around him—the smoke filters in the room didn't seem to be working. He toyed with a stack of microfiche in front of him, checked one of the screens (a view of the hall outside: a bored guard was relating a story to another with extravagant and obscene gestures), and looked down at Potok. He bit on his lower lip in concentration.

"Representative Potok," he said languidly, his voice just this side of boredom, "Gunnar had been contracted to be killed by the Hoorka—as you well know—and the Hoorka are bound by their guild bylaws not to release the name involved in their unsuccessful attempts *and* to make public the signer of successful assassinations. I suggest you make your plea to Hoorka, and not the Assembly, if you are so interested in learning the identity—or perhaps you might advise Gunnar to run slower next time."

A roar of laughter rose from guild-members allied with

Vingi, coupled with derisive boos from Gunnar's supporters.

"M'Dame Ricia Cuscratti was not killed by Hoorka," insisted Potok.

Vingi waved pudgy fingers in dismissal. "There is no proof of *that* beyond vague rumors; in any event, sirrah, m'Dame Cuscratti's murderers will be fined to the limits of the law should their identities come to light, and your guild-kin may demand bloodfeud if m'Dame Cuscratti's guild-kin do not insist upon preference. I fail to see the point of your persistence."

There was a murmuring of affirmation from the floor, a bee-hum that filled the hall with wordless clamor. Potok raised his eyes to the sun-brightened windows above him and waited for silence. The noise died slowly and incompletely.

"The attempted killing of Gunnar might well be a cause for bloodfeud between our guild and another," he continued. "And we have a right to know what lies behind the attempt, whether it was a personal insult or a matter for all of Gunnar's kin—my kin. If, for instance, a part of our government were trying to gain total control of this Assembly"—he paused significantly—"or attempting to consolidate what they already control, then the guilds would have a right to know."

A shout of contempt came from the left side of the hall, joined by a few other voices. "Sit down, Potok! You're interrupting—"

As Potok turned to deal with the hecklers, his own supporters voiced their own feelings at suitable volume. The contention rose, the voices growing steadily louder and more numerous as members of the ruling guilds joined in on one side or another. Potok, his chest heaving, struggled to be heard above them, facing Vingi and bellowing his complaints. Vingi sat watching the disturbance, then raised the gavel of office. He let the gavel fall and the amplified thud of wood on wood rang throughout the hall; a low, ringing note. The discussions faded slowly. Potok bowed to Vingi. "My thanks, Li-Gallant."

"I simply didn't care to see the hall in dissension,

Representative. I wouldn't think it would behoove you to see it so, either. Will you yield the floor *now*, sirrah?"

Potok shook his head. He shuffled the papers on his desk, glancing up to the dais. "I do not. There are other questions I would like answered, if the Li-Gallant has no answer to the others I've asked. Our sources, for one, tell us that certain parties have been selling ippicator skeletons to offworld concerns without paying the proper tithes to the guild treasuries, and without the tax that is due Neweden. Is that true?"

"If your sources are reliable, but the government has heard nothing of this. I will investigate it personally. Does that satisfy you, sirrah?"

"I trust the report will be prompt, Li-Gallant, since ippicator skeletons are a finite resource, and once depleted cannot be restored. Another matter: our guild-kin in Illi say that their continent has not been receiving its entire stipend for food, and that lassari have actually starved in Illicata. The ore mines have provided ore for the factories, the fishermen have produced record catches, and the farmers of the Southern Plain have had adequate rainfall this season. How can they not be prospering? Yet the figures I have before me"—he waved a sheet of flimsies about—"show an interesting dichotomy. I would like to read these into the record . . ."

"The government of Neweden is not interested in fiction, Representative Potok. Your kin in Illi are not members of this Assembly by vote of the guilds. Representative Heenan of Illi *is*. I suggest you go over the figures with him and let us get on with more pressing business." Vingi turned deliberately away from Potok, his ringed fingers spitting light as they passed through a stray sunbeam. Again shouts of agreement and protest came from the floor. Potok screamed to be heard.

"*I will not yield the floor until this Assembly listens to me!*"

He was shouted down. Across the floor, representatives rose to their feet to be better heard. Several strident voices demanded the floor as members of contending guilds exchanged taunts and threats. The pounding of the gavel was heard and ignored, and Vingi shouted for order into a nearby microphone, his voice ragged with overamplification. The noise quieted somewhat, but did not die. Potok crossed his arms over his chest and faced the dais with a face gray with anger. "I demand to be heard, Li-Gallant."

"You've been heard for the last hour, sirrah. Will you yield?" Wearily, for Vingi was genuinely tired. His rump hurt, his right foot itched, and he was beginning to feel faint hunger.

"I will not. I have the floor. I intend to keep it until I receive some satisfaction. I'll talk all day if necessary. The leader of my guild has been nearly killed, and the current government ignores the people it supposedly serves."

"You needn't slander this Assembly in the hall, in open meeting." Vingi's voice boomed through the speakers, dwarfing that of Potok.

"Slander is sometimes truth," Potok said harshly, his voice showing the strain of constant shouting. Behind him, others of his guild clamored agreement. The holocameras filming the session moved from the over-righteous face of Potok to the thick features of Vingi.

The Li-Gallant's double chin trembled as he pointed to Potok with a forefinger. "You had better be prepared to back up such libel with facts, Representative, if only for the sake of your kin. Do you understand me, sirrah?" From the Li-Gallant, the honorific sounded like an insult. "We've heard more than enough of your vague references to troubles of which we're already fully aware. For the last time, will you yield the floor? There are others waiting to be heard, with problems perhaps more urgent than your own."

Shouts of "Sit down!" now alternated with yells of support for Potok, a cacophony that caused the birds on the dome to once more rise from their nests and flutter about. The gavel boomed unsuccessfully as Potok stood with his arms still folded, waiting for quiet to return. The tumult continued, the gavel booming repeatedly until it finally wore down the opposition. Vingi spoke as soon as he felt he could be heard.

"A final warning, Representative Potok. Sit down and yield the floor, or I'll be compelled to call for the sergeant-at-arms to remove you from the hall. I don't make that threat lightly, sirrah."

Potok took a prolonged sip from the glass of water on his desk, feeling the cool liquid soothe his ragged throat. He swallowed, taking his time and trying to gauge the growing ire of the Li-Gallant. Finally, he placed the glass carefully on his desk and shuffled his papers into order, holding them in one hand and raising them to the multi-colored windows above. "I cannot in conscience yield, Li-Gallant. There is importance in what I'm saying, and if the Assembly won't hear me willingly, then let it suffer."

He brought the papers down before him, cleared his throat, and began reading from the first sheet as once more the riotous clangor of protest rose. Potok continued reading, seemingly undisturbed, though his voice was no longer audible. Papers were scattered from a desk to the rear of the hall as two representatives argued furiously. Vingi didn't bother to use the gavel, but gestured to the guards behind him. They moved through the aisles toward Potok; he, seeing their approach, continued reading as the uproar raged about him. The guards reached him, and Potok threw the papers into the air in dramatic disgust as they forced him away from his desk, finally pinning his arms to his side and carrying him when he refused to walk before them. The papers fell, autumnal. They were trampled onto the hall floor underfoot as the guards bore Potok to the doors leading from the hall. The noise rose decibels louder, and the gavel rose and fell unheeded. The great doors of the hall opened and swallowed the trio of guards and Potok. Birds flew in uneasy circles outside the dome.

In her office in the Diplo Center, m'Dame d'Embry watched a holotank set temporarily in the center of her room. There, in miniature, the Assembly Hall teemed with furiously gesticulating figures and a dull, inarticulate roar filled the speakers under the 'tank. Stretching forth an orange-tinted arm to the controls on her desk, the Alliance Regent turned down the volume with a sharp movement of her wrist. She shook her head, lips pursed, and then turned to her own work.

A procession of the Dead walked outward from the Sterka Gates, into the roadway that hugged the hill ridges of the plain beyond. The fumes of their incense were smeared behind them by the easterly wind and their chanting—a dull and sibilant mantra—lulled the Neweden breeze into submission and put the sunstar to sleep. In darkness, they made their aimless, sorrowful way through the countryside; unseeing, uncaring.

A man in ragged clothing toppled in their midst, falling to the hard-packed surface of the road. The Dead ignored him, though the chant changed subtly into a praise for the presence of Hag Death. The man groaned in pain as he clutched his side. If the Dead that passed saw the blood from a vibro gash that stained his clothing, they took no notice.

What did it matter how Hag Death arranged to take a person? All would go to Her in time.

Five

It was another local and petty bloodfeud.

Jast Claswell, a wealthy kin of the Bard's Guild, wished to dispose of his wife's lover, a problem compounded by the fact that his wife had had the bad taste to choose a lover outside the guild. The problem was common enough on any world, and common on Neweden. Kinship made for further difficulties. Claswell, a native of the Illian continent, had contacted the Hoorka rather than demanding personal satisfaction. The Hoorka price was normally too high for such domestic vendettas, but Claswell had recently come into possession of a cache of ippicator skeletons and had sold them to an offworld trader without going through the normal Neweden channels, thus avoiding the heavy tax on ippicator relics. It meant that he had monies to use as he wished, and his wish was to kill the man that made him a cuckold.

The apprentices had offered the alternatives to the potential victim, Enus Dausset, but the man couldn't match the fee and thus negate the contract. Five hours before the Underasgard sunset, Dausset was given the traditional warning, and a dye containing a trace of radioactive material was splashed on his arm; it could not easily be washed off and would remain active for several hours, allowing the apprentices to track the man until the Hoorka assassins arrived. A watch was set around Dausset's home —it was mid-afternoon on that part of the Illian continent.

All this unfolded while the Thane and Aldhelm slept in

Underasgard. For such routines, apprentices were sufficient.

An hour before the sun dropped behind the cliff fronting the main entrance to the Hoorka caverns, word came to Underasgard that Dausset had purchased a handlaser from a weapons store. Bodyshields were set out and the two Hoorka awakened. Final reports drifted in as they prepared to leave the caverns and fly to Illi. Dausset had secretly paid a last visit to Claswell's wife (the Thane found himself admiring the man's courage and/or foolishness in doing that). Dausset had headed south from the city of Irast. Dausset had turned west by south and fled toward the tumbled ridges of the Twisted Hills. After the last report, rope and heavy footgear were added to the assassin's equipment.

During the flight in the Hoorka-owned hovercraft, Aldhelm and the Thane confined their speech to generalities, and when the craft landed near the edge of the Twisted Hills, they simply unloaded their equipment and watched as the aircraft blinked its landing lights in salute and left them. Around the two, the hills were silvered in the light of Neweden's double moons, Gulltopp and Sleipnir. The night held the chill of the approaching winter and both the Thane and Aldhelm kept their nightcloaks wrapped tightly about them as some protection against the breeze. A few nightstalkers mewled and shrieked their various hunting cries to the cold air, but otherwise the landscape was a barren panorama of shattered rock and broken ground, the remnants of some ancient cataclysm.

"What did that last report say?" The Thane scanned the empty slopes, seeing nothing but the unmoving, scraggling desert brush that clung precariously to the few pockets of soil. The night, for all its briskness, was arid. The Thane's throat was dry, as if the air had leached him of inner moisture. He cleared his throat in irritation. After the noise of the flight, the silence was a palpable presence. His voice had sounded dead and weak.

Aldhelm squinted into darkness and waited a long minute before he answered the Thane. "The apprentices swear he's hidden himself in the foothills a few kilometers south of here. I have the bearings." He swung his hand in the indicated direction, his nightcloak rustling. To the Thane, Aldhelm was a deeper darkness against the sky, his flesh shadowed and his mouth concealed in the folds of his cloak. Only his eyes and the crusted wound on his upper cheek were clearly visible. That bothered the Thane—it briefly occurred to him that Aldhelm might be trying to make the wound more conspicuous, knowing it would irritate the Thane—but the Thane was himself bundled in a similar fashion. *Your fears are taking over your logic. Stop trying to rationalize every small detail.*

The Thane checked the gear in the pouch of his nightcloak, loosened his vibro in its sheath, and checked the power of his bodyshield.

"Well, kin-brother," he said, "what do you suggest we do?" The Thane yawned and shivered.

"Go around the man. He expects us from the direction of the port in Irast, in all likelihood. It'll be simpler if we can come in unseen from the opposite direction. I doubt that he has any idea where our craft left us."

"Good." Even as he said it, the Thane knew that his response was wrong. It sounded patronizing and belittling; as the question, in essence, had been. It was a question the least schooled apprentice could have answered, and it spoke well of Aldhelm's forebearance that he even deigned to speak. And he spoke now with feeling.

"I'm not an apprentice or journeyman, Thane. I haven't your age or experience, but I've been your kin for some time, if you recall." Aldhelm's voice was haughty and righteously angry. The words cut into the Thane as if edged.

Aldhelm stared into the shadowed valleys of the hills. He scuffed his feet at the dirt in impatience, not looking at the Thane. "The night isn't eternal, Thane, and Hag Death waits Her due. Let's go."

"Not until we settle this. Speak your mind. We can spare the time, and I think it more important than the contract."

"This contract is less important than Gunnar's? What of your—our—code, Thane? Each contract is as important as the next."

"It was a poor choice of words." Wearily, but with impatience. "What bothers you, Aldhelm?"

"You don't know?" His voice sounded genuinely surprised. Aldhelm turned to face the Thane, eyes glinting in the darkness of his face. When he next spoke, his words were harsh and bitter, as if the taste of them burned his tongue. "Why did you pull me from the rotation? Wasn't it enough that I failed the Gunnar contract, or don't you think I'm capable of realizing the import of my mistake? Don't you think I chastised myself far more harshly than you ever could?"

Gulltopp, the smaller of the moons, was setting behind Aldhelm, and its brass-gold light shimmered around him and glazed the hills. "I came close to breaking the damned code, knowing the reactions to Gunnar's escape. I could have killed Gunnar, just seconds after dawn. But I held back—I have that much respect for what the code has done for my kin; I respect Dame Fate and She of the Five Limbs that much. But I should have followed my instincts. No one would have seen, no one but the Gods would have known. Not even you. If I were able to return to that moment . . ."

He paused, then continued with an agonized hurt in his voice that lashed at the Thane. "Do you have to give me further humiliation by treating me like some rank nouveau?" He uttered a short, caustic expletive as the edge of Gulltopp touched the peaks of the Twisted Hills.

The Thane met Aldhelm's gaze. Neither flinched or looked away.

"What did you expect?" asked the Thane. "I had to emphasize to all Hoorka-kin the precariousness of our position in this power struggle between the Li-Gallant and Gunnar. The fact that I'd found it necessary to discipline *you*, the most competent Hoorka I have, man or woman, will carry much weight. It's the most convincing evidence that we're innocent of conspiring with Gunnar. I don't want Hoorka involved in a bloodfeud between guilds, and I won't let us be dragged into the Assembly and outlawed. Anything such as that would jeopardize our chances of growing, of going offworld or escaping Neweden. Gunnar and Vingi will play their power games, and I won't let Hoorka be a pawn on that board." *So simplistic*, he thought. *The words don't even convince me. What can they do for Aldhem except to convince him that I don't care for him; as a friend, as kin?*

Aldhelm spread his hands wide in the dying light of Gulltopp. "So I'm reduced to being an example in your textbook?" His words quivered with suppressed menace, and for the first time the Thane was aware of the other's sheer bulk, of his physical conditioning and sharper skills. In the Thane's younger days, he could have taken Aldhelm, or at least he flattered himself to think so, but now . . . He was no longer sure, and were there a physical confrontation, Aldhelm would most likely best the Thane. The realization did little to comfort the older man.

But Aldhelm suddenly swept his hand through the cold air in aimless, undirected disgust, breaking their locked gazes as he turned to stare moodily at the surrounding hills as if they were mocking strangers tittering at the Hoorka's overheard conversation.

The Thane placed a hand on Aldhelm's shoulder and forced the Hoorka to look at him. "Aldhelm, I've considered you to be my most likely successor, and I've considered you to be more than a simple kin-brother. You're the best of the kin, more accomplished than I ever was. But I'd throw you to Vingi's guards tied hand and foot if I thought it would save Hoorka. My life is Hoorka's. As is yours. I won't have us destroyed, no matter what sacrifice is demanded. Do you understand?" There was no sympathy there, no hint of the doubts he felt inside. The Thane spoke with an iron voice tempered and made steel, the voice he'd used in the past when he'd taken a ragged band of lassari and by force of personality and fighting prowess had turned them into the Hoorka—a voice he hadn't used in standards. The words echoed faintly among the stones of the hills.

Aldhelm glanced at the Thane's hand and brushed it away ungently. "I understand better than you may think," he said.

Aldhelm turned and began moving into the tortured land of the hills, the sparse night dew from the brush beading on the hem of his nightcloak as Gulltopp sank fully below the horizon. The light in the hills changed suddenly, becoming more bluish and cold, as only Sleipnir was left to wander among the stars. Aldhelm, one foot on a fallen boulder, suddenly thrust himself up and pivoted, facing the Thane again. "I understand your reasoning and your motives. As to your claim of friendship, I don't believe you capable of it. Nor would Mondom, I think. You're too reserved a man for that, my kin-brother, too much in love with your creation. No, your love is reserved for a thing, not for people. You care for the words that bind Hoorka, not for the kin that form our guild, and your affection is cold and dry." He walked a few steps away from the Thane. "And I hope that disturbs you," he said to the rocky landscape before them.

The Thane, his thoughts a maelstrom both contradictory and painful, watched Aldhelm move away into the Hills, finally disappearing from sight around a cliff that held back the heights from the broken ground below. He listened to the quiet around him. Finally, with a violent start, he followed the path Aldhelm had taken.

Fulfillment of the contract was simple, routine.

The Thane wondered if he should not have left the task to the apprentices to hone their skills. They found Dausset sitting on a rock below a ledge not far into the hills, looking toward the glow on the horizon that bespoke the presence of Irast. The man's head moved slowly from side to side as he swept the plains for signs of movement, but he never looked to the slope behind him nor saw the two Hoorka suddenly appear against the sky and stare down at him from the heights. The barrel of his weapon glistened harshly in Sleipnir's light. Dausset coughed once, a sound startlingly loud in the night. The Thane and Aldhelm studied the man, and their sensors picked up the mark of the apprentices' dye on him. The Thane nodded to Aldhelm.

The younger Hoorka kicked a pebble downslope and, as Dausset turned toward the noise, threw his dagger with seeming nonchalance. It sped true. Dausset grunted in surprise, then crumpled without further outcry, the hand laser unused. Blood stained the rocks beneath him. Quite quickly, quite simply, it was over. The assassins made their way to where the body lay.

"Good work, Aldhelm."

Aldhelm disdained to reply.

The Thane shrugged. "Turn him over. I want to look at him."

"Doesn't the fourth code-line state that the Hoorka must show no concern for the victim, must consider him to be wed to Hag Death once the warning is given so we feel no pity?"

There was mockery in Aldhelm's voice. The Thane ignored it. "A minor quirk, that's all. I like to see their faces, to know how the souls I send to the gods appeared in this life." *No, that's not the truth. This sudden concern with appearances started only recently, when the faceless dead began crowding your dreams. Are you . . .* The Thane cut off the inner contention with a physical wrench. "Turn him over," he repeated, with self-irritation evident in his voice. He doubted that Aldhelm would notice the inward direction of his contempt.

Aldhelm shrugged and turned the body with his foot. Moonlight washed the contorted features of the man's face and outlined the edges of the death-rictus. A thick rivulet of blood trickled from the corner of his mouth and across his right cheek. Thin and unmuscular hands clasped his useless weapon. Dausset's was a common face, a crowd face: thin but not exceedingly so, eyes set a shade too close to a bony and inelegant nose. The Thane wondered what the woman had seen in him to violate her contract with a wealthy man. He reached down and turned off Aldhelm's vibro before pulling it from the wound. It came forth easily, with more blood following; bright, arterial blood. The Thane handed the blade to the Hoorka. Aldhelm plunged it once into the earth to cleanse it—feeding She of the Five Limbs—and placed it back in his sheath.

"Let's finish this."

They wrapped the body in an extra nightcloak and began the long trek back to Claswell's dwelling. The body, a limp weight, swung loosely between the two.

It was still early night when they passed the Irast city gates—two huge doors of black malawood swung to and secured, a symbolic defense. The taverns just inside the gates were full of drinking customers and the shops still had their display windows open to the streets, holos flaring above them in a visual cacophony. The lanes and pedestrian ways were crowded, but all moved aside for the Hoorka and their burden. Faces turned from the business of buying and selling, the more curious following for a time, though no one attempted to hinder them. No sane person would insult Hoorka-kin. Once they passed a band of jussar, young ruffians as yet unattached to any guild but too young to be termed lassari. Their bare chests glittered with fluorescent patterns and vibros hung conspicuously at their sides, but they, too, let the Hoorka pass. The assassins walked slowly, without speaking, their eyes glaring at the path ahead and not to the gathering crowd behind them. The people of Irast, after a curious stare, moved quickly aside.

When they finally deposited the body of Dausset at the gate of Claswell's home, they had attracted a sizable number of the denizens of Irastian nightlife. There were scattered catcalls directed to the opaqued windows of the Claswell manse; cries of amused derision, for Irast was a small town and many were privy to this particular piece of gossip. The crowd, rapidly growing larger and more pleased with its attempts at wit, parted to let the assassins by as the Hoorka turned to go, then closed in again. They clamored excitedly around the corpse and hooted their contempt for Claswell's cowardice in the face of cuckoldry. As they began to pound at the gates and a ragged chorus began—a popular song with the words altered to suit the situation by some quick mind in the crowd—the Hoorka left, as calm and unemotionally as they'd come.

(For is it not the sixth code-line that states that the signer of a fulfilled contract be made a matter of public knowledge—that the Hoorka will hide the identity of neither slayer nor slain? For the Hoorka are but weapons in the hands of another, and the murder will not lie before their conscience, but that of the contractor. And it is also true that the contractor may himself become the subject of a Hoorka contract. Revenge is a powerful emotion.)

The Thane and Aldhelm spoke of nothing but trivialities during their return to Underasgard. After eating and bathing, they retired to their rooms to sleep. The Thane's rest was fitful. Spectres without faces haunted his dreams. And then there were faces: his own face, an old, old visage channeled and furrowed by too much time; he danced a macabre arabesque with the swollen and malevolent mask of Vingi in the dank caverns of the ippicator. Vingi laughed at the odd appearance of the five-legged beast, mocking it as an animal unfit to live, unsuited to its environment and unable to cope with change. Then, together, they smashed the skeleton to broken dust. And in the darkness, he could hear the giggling mirth of Hag Death.

The spires of the Port were gilded by the early sun. Far off on the flattened expanse of earth that served as Neweden's link to the worlds of the Alliance, ground vehicles bore the phallic cylinders of storage units to the waiting freighters at the edge of the landing field. To one side of the Port stood the buildings of Sterka—nearest the Port; the hostels, the bars, and places of varied entertainment for the crews of the Alliance ships coming in and out of Neweden. Across the field from the city stood the ornate and intricate architecture of the Diplo Center. It was a varied if not beautiful scene by morning, and m'Dame d'Embry, the Alliance Regent of the Diplos on Neweden, gazed long at it before opaquing the window and turning back into her rooms.

She often compared Neweden to Niffleheim, and Neweden sometimes had the best of the comparison. Neweden had the rough grace of untilled and little-known regions to recommend it, a crude pastorality that the more urban and urbane worlds lacked. Crowded worlds and aesthetics that turned to dry dust in the eyes seemed to go together—it had been decades since she had been awed by the sight of Niffleheim's metallic surface.

The room had already taken the sleeping plate to the ceiling, where the plate functioned as a lighting unit. Music drifted in polyphonic eddies from the walls—a harpsichord concerto by Hagee, an obscure Terran composer—and a holo of d'Vellia's soundsculpture *Gehennah*, half-size, loomed in the corner nearest the comlink. In her dressing gown and without the bodytints that had once been fashionable (and which she still wore, unaware or simply uncaring that they were no longer in favor), her body reflected its age. The eyes were caught up in a finely-knit spiderweb of lines, her face had a patina of grayness, and when she moved it was with a certain sureness that is missing in a younger person's step, the kittenish ungainliness of youth. She didn't bother to treat her hair—it was dry and whitened. The flesh on her body had a laxness, a sag, as if it had once confined more bulk than she now possessed. But if d'Embry had lost physical fullness, she was compensated by an arid spirit; as if in leaving, the flesh had cast off and left behind the energy it once encompassed. The snared eyes were undimmed and lively, the gnarled hands strong and agile. She was a legend in Diplo circles, the grand-dame of Niffleheim, and she had resisted all well-meaning attempts to retire her from active duty with a fervor that had impressed, awed, and irritated the Niffleheim authorities. As a Diplo, she was effective; as a political in-fighter, without peer.

And she was nearing the end. Inside, she knew it. Perhaps another ten standards before the drugs, implants, and mechanical aids could no longer keep that body together. That gave her drive, and if she was occasionally brusque and quick, she attributed it—in her mind—to that fact. She had little time to waste on foolishness.

"Comlink," she said to the empty room.

"M'Dame?" The screen of the comlink flared and settled into a blue-gray background that flickered slightly. D'Embry moved to the mechanism and, running her hands across the keyboard there, pressed a button. Light surged and letters raced across the screen. "Neweden status bank," chimed the comlink in a neuter voice, echoing redundantly the words printed on the screen.

"Report from local time 21:30 to the present. I want an emphasis on governmental problems. Briefly. You know what I'm after."

The comlink voice changed to a woman's contralto, evidently that of a staff Diplo. "M'Dame, one moment please."

"Certainly." D'Embry tapped the carpet of the room with one bare foot, noticing that the carpet needed to be trimmed again—it had grown too high for her liking. She made a mental note to have the Maintenance Department groom the rug.

"Sorry for the delay, m'Dame. I note here that at 22:00, the Li-Gallant received a committee of guild-members sympathetic to his guild's rule." The woman's voice continued as an accompanying text appeared on the screen. "Topic of their discussion is unknown, but the conjecture is that it concerned consolidation of support after the Assembly meeting of yesterday afternoon. Query?"

"No." D'Embry's voice was dry, and she cleared her throat. "Continue, please."

"22:15. Gunnar and Potok were seen in the pastures of their guild holdings outside Sterka. They refused to speak to the news services. Query?"

"No. Give me a general update, quickly." She used a side panel of the comlink to order her breakfast, then asked the room to elevate a chair. She sat, then spoke as the woman on the link began to speak again. "Cancel that last request. My mind's already cluttered with enough useless facts for the day. What of the Hoorka?"

"We understand that they fulfilled a contract last night in Irast. A copy of the completed contract was sent to the Center from Underasgard in compliance with your request. Query?"

"Put the contract on visual, please." D'Embry scanned the contract without truly reading it. She glanced at the names of contractor and victim, her lips pursed in a moue of distaste, but the names were simply a random arrangement of letters that meant nothing to her. Her fingertips tapped the console of the comlink. The gray paint was worn to bare metal where her hands rested. "Negate," she said, and the screen cleared.

"Please come on visual yourself," she said. The screen flickered and then filled with the head and shoulders of a young woman, her hair short at the sides and long down her back in current fashion, her eyelids and lips touched with a faint scarlet sheen that seemed to burn with a tepid fire. "Ahh, Stanee," d'Embry said. "Good morning."

The face smiled. "Thank you, m'Dame. Anything else I can do for you?"

D'Embry waved the question away. "I hate the coldness of the words on the screen after a while, so you'll excuse the visual contact. I simply get an urge, now and again, to see to whom I'm talking. A whim, child, nothing more."

Stanee's smile remained fixed. It seemed the predominant feature of her face. "Certainly, m'Dame."

"Do you have the figures for Sterka last night?—not the gory facts that get attached to them in this barbaric place, just the figures. And I'll probably ask you to stop halfway through them, so don't be overly perturbed at your record-keeping being unappreciated."

Stanee looked down, below the camera's view. The head and shoulders on the screen moved as her fingers raced over controls. Without looking up, she began reading. "Sterka continent: killed by bloodfeud, three. Assaults, twenty. Incidents that might lead to guild conflicts, four reported . . ." The list went on, number after number sifted from the chaff of the night.

"Enough," d'Embry interrupted finally. She sigh-smiled and shook her head at Stanee. "Enough for now. Did it ever occur to you that this is a world with damnably little to recommend it—with the exception of ippicator skeletons and some pretty but unspectacular scenery? Ahh, never mind, never mind." She waved a hand in the air. "Just the normal morning grumpiness. Have a flimsy sent to my office to look over later, will you? You can cram into it all those boring details that I know you've been dying to give me, neh?"

Dutiful laughter. "Yes, m'Dame. Is that all?"

"For now. End," she said in a less personal tone of voice. The comlink cleared to a blank blue-gray. "Off." The screen darkened and went black as it eased into its niche in the wall, out of sight.

D'Embry went to the window and cleared it again. The sun had risen higher in the sky, pursued by high cumulus clouds, and the light had gone from the honey-thick yellow of the dawn to the whiter, more penetrating glare of full day. The buildings basked in warmth, throwing sharp-edged shadows across the plain of the Port. A freighter rose, its attitude jets throwing off hot gases to waver the air. The ship hovered low over the Port for a moment, and then arced into the Neweden morning, leaving a dirty trail that the wind wiped across the sky. In the city, dark specks of birds wheeled in alarm.

The Port was alive with workers and Alliance personnel beginning a new day. For them, another day of relative sameness. The daily problems came and went without ever being eliminated.

M'Dame d'Embry sighed deep within herself and slapped at the window controls. She watched the glass turn slowly smoky and then deep purple-black, inking out the view of the Port. She leaned against the wall in reverie for a moment or two, forcing her mind to come to full alertness. Finally, rather desultorily, she began to dress.

The sun warmed the soil of the hills, but the heat and light of the sunstar failed to disturb the cool night that lingered below ground. The caverns of Underasgard, eternally cloaked and ever-mild, paid little attention to the vagaries of the surface.

For Hoorka-kin, however, the rising sun heralded a Rites Day, a day full with the worship of their patron gods. Kin spoke quietly to one another, the kitchens served only cold bread and milk, and the apprentices were kept busy ensuring that all nightcloaks were pressed and clean. A hurried calm held the caverns, a busy laziness. The Hoorka gathered slowly in the Chamber, the largest of the caverns they inhabited, and took their seats before the High Altar.

The Thane, sitting to the utter rear of the Chamber, watched the assembly as if rapt. His mind, however, dwelt elsewhere. He was only marginally aware of Mondom's warmth at his side, of Cranmer's fidgeting, of Aldhelm's curt greetings. He distantly nodded to the journeymen and apprentices as they entered. When the ponderous chords of the chant of praise rose, his lips mouthed the words and his voice sang, but he heard nothing.

"I love the feel of your body." Mondom smiled, faint lines appearing at the corners of her mouth. Teasing, her eyes danced.

The Thane rolled over on his back so that her roving hands had access to all of him. His gaze moved from her face and down the lean tautness of Mondom's body. He stroked the upper swell of her breasts softly, and smiled as her eyes closed.

"Damn you," she said, a velvet growl, and her hand found him. Laughing, they kissed. Still laughing, she straddled him.

The chanters had finished the descant. Ric d'Mannberg began a short reading from the annals of She of the Five Limbs, one of the more violent passages. His droning voice spoke of kin slaying kin, of disembowelments and cannibalism. The Thane woke from his reverie and found Cranmer engrossed in the account of She. "You find this fascinating, scholar?" he whispered.

Cranmer leaned toward the Thane, whispering in return. "Only in the sheer number of gods with which Neweden, for all her poverty, is, ahh, blessed with having. It's staggering. All the various guilds, and few of them sharing the same patrons . . . Neweden must have been a crowded world during the days of these gods."

"Until She of the Five Limbs banished most."

"For an ippicator, even one of such power, that must have been an amazing feat." Cranmer glanced at the Altar, where d'Mannberg had closed the book and nodded in salutation. "And I notice that your attention wanders, Thane. I'm curious—your true—father was an offworlder by birth, and came to Neweden's religions as a convert. Do you believe, or is it simply convenient?"

"Do you have faith, Cranmer?"

"In gods? No."

"Too bad." The Thane leaned back in his seat, closing his eyes again. D'Mannberg opened the Annals once more. His voice droned on.

His real parents, lassari, had brought the boy to Hoorka. The Thane had glared down at the thin, wiry child of . . . thirteen? And the boy had glared back, uncowed. The Thane had liked the defiance of the child and took the young Aldhelm as kin. The parents, over-grateful, and perhaps pleased to be rid of the extra mouth, had taken a quick leave. They had never again inquired after their son. He now had kin—parents were unimportant.

"Watch your opponent's hips," he'd said to the new apprentice one day, during a training session. "Other parts

of the body may feint—the legs, the arms, the head, the eyes. But where the hips go, the body must follow."

Aldhelm shook his head. His hands toying with the hilt of his vibro, he'd stared at the Thane. "No, that seems wrong. I watch the hands and feet. They do the damage."

"You don't have four eyes to watch each."

"Two are sufficient."

Something in the boy's stubbornness and insistence touched a response in the Thane. He'd stripped and joined the youngster on the practice floor. "Defend yourself, then," he'd said. He circled the apprentice, watching the vibro and the hips. It took much longer than he'd anticipated—the Thane was slick with sweat when they'd finished—but he found the flaws in Aldhelm's defense, disarmed and pinned the boy to the floor of Underasgard. Still, he was impressed by Aldhelm's raw, untutored skill.

"You see," he said, getting to his feet and releasing the boy. "Had you watched me correctly, that would not have happened. In a fight, you'd have been very dead, boy, despite your thoughts on what to watch."

"I'll think about it, sirrah." That was as much admission as Aldhelm would give the Thane.

The dance to Hag Death had begun. Brilliant in scarlet robes and satin ribbons, blue hairplumes bobbing with movement, the dancers circled each other. Steel blades in their hands glinted in the lights. A sackbutt snorted a chorus, joined by a trio of recorders. There were two dancers of each sex, and their bare feet slapped the stones of Underasgard as they went through the ritualistic steps, a choreographed battle representing the strife between Dame Fate and the Hag. Blades flashed and met, clashing with a faint, bell-like ringing.

The bells for evening meals had just rung. Aldhelm had brought the Thane's dinner to him, dismissing the apprentice that usually performed that task. He sat the tray on the Thane's table, setting the controls to "warm" so that the meat remained hot. Fragrant vapors filled the room.

"Aldhelm?" the Thane said in some surprise. "Since when do you perform apprentice's tasks? You're nearly a full Hoorka."

"I had a favor to ask, a boon." His voice, usually so confident, was slow and unsure, halting.

"Ask, then."

A hesitation. "You'll sponsor me for my mastership in the Hoorka, be my kin-father?" Aldhelm said the words in a rush, the words falling over each other in their haste to leave his mouth. But his eyes—they held the Thane, and there was open affection there, and an unusual vulnerability that was foreign to Aldhelm.

Knowing what he was going to say, that openness hurt the Thane more than he thought possible.

"I've never sponsored any journeyman, Aldhelm." He said the words slowly, hoping that Aldhelm might reconsider and withdraw the request himself, and knowing that it wouldn't happen that way.

Aldhelm frowned. He looked down at the floor and then up to the Thane. "I realize that. That's why I've waited so long to ask." A vague smile touched his lips. "You've spoken well of me, and we like each other. I would *like your sponsoring. It would mean much to me."*

"I"—a pause—"can't."

Aldhelm was stoic. His stance was as erect as before, his body betraying no disappointment. Yet something had changed: his eyes were guarded now, and perhaps too moist.

The Thane hastened to explain. "If there were *a journeyman I would take as kin-son, it would be you, Aldhelm. Truly. But I don't care to have the Hoorka become like other guilds, where the kin-son of the guild ruler inherits his father's position. The best Hoorka should always rule Hoorka, and all the kin should have some say in who governs them. If I were to name a son or daughter, it would be a statement, an indication of favoritism. It's easier if I simply avoid that."*

The Thane stared at Aldhelm, but the young man simply gazed back at him, his eyes unreadable and untouchable. "Do you understand? Aldhelm, I don't wish to hurt you—as I said, were I to sponsor anyone . . ."

"I understand, Thane." Aldhelm shrugged and began to leave the room.

"Aldhelm . . ."

"Yah?" The Hoorka turned and faced the Thane.

"What of Bronton? He admires your skill as much as I, and he is well-liked among the kin. He would sponsor you, and it would be to your credit."

"Thank you for your concern, Thane." Again, the shrugging of shoulders. A smile came and vanished, tentative. "I'll ask him." And with that, Aldhelm turned and left.

The Thane stared at the tray of food on his table for long minutes before beginning to eat.

The dancers, in a flourish of weapons, left the dais. A journeywoman attired in saffron robes intoned the benediction. An audible sigh crossed the Chamber, and with a rustling of cloth, the Hoorka-kin rose and began to leave. The Thane stretched and rose as Cranmer and Mondom stood beside him.

"He slept well, didn't he, Mondom?" Cranmer placed his hands below his head in imitation of a pillow and closed his eyes.

"Our Thane?" Mondom smiled. "He has an excuse, having taken the contract last night."

"Both of you are mistaken. I simply concentrate better with my eyes closed. Prayer, after all, is a mental effort. Neh, scholar?" The Thane yawned, involuntarily, then joined in with the laughter of the other two.

Six

A large gathering had crowded *en masse* before the Assembly Hall after marching noisily from Tri-Unity Square. A few flat-signs proclaimed various guilds' support of one obscure issue or another, but the guards ranked on the steps to the Hall didn't bother to read them, being all too used to such displays. Protests of one variety or another were commonplace enough on Neweden since the advent of the All-Guild Assembly created by Li-Gallant Perrin, the current Li-Gallant's kin-father. The week before, it had been a group of ore farmers from Nean that had staged a minor riot in the capital city of that continent during the Li-Gallant's visit. Several demonstrators had been incarcerated, and more were injured in the fighting that came when the security people attempted to disperse them. It was not, however, an unusual occurrence except in the number of injuries.

Where guilds and pride were concerned, tempers flared easily but carefully—the offended person might be a better fighter than you. Most demonstrations were noisy but well-behaved. After their time of shouting and preening for the news services, the crowds faded and died, the people melting back into the streets.

So the guards watched with a bored and uninterested demeanor as the vanguard of the protestors edged to the base of the steps. A chant was shouted in ragged unison, though no words could be easily discerned. Two beats—a strong accent followed by a weaker one, then a pause—a waltz protest. The signs moved with the chant, upraised to the sunstar in the phosphorus zenith.

One guard fidgeted in his pockets, pulling forth a packet of mildly intoxicating candies from the south coast. He offered one to the nearest companion.

The chant of the crowd waxed and ebbed, a tide-swell that moved in its own rhythm, a thousand-throated beast wailing distress to the silent facade of the Hall. Few details stood out in the Brownian motion of the protesters: a flash of iridescent cloth; a person near the front, taller by a head than his neighbors and further individualized by a spiked plant-pet growing like a living collar around his neck; the uneven summits of the signs pooling thin shadows on those below. The far edge of the crowd was not sharply defined, but faded into a perimeter consisting equally of interested but unmotivated spectators and those using the demonstration as an excuse for play—youngsters running happily through the legs of adults; streetkids, jussar.

Had it been like the hundred protests before it, this would have been a short-lived commingling that would have died quickly from the lack of response from the Hall and the failure of the Neweden news services to arrive (the holo networks had been prudently notified by the march's organizers, but knowing Vingi's present mood, had declined the offer).

But the former demonstrations didn't have the Nean "riot" and the furor of the Assembly meeting the day before. These gnawed at Vingi's thin tolerance for opposition. The guards had been sternly instructed to disperse and scatter any large gatherings before the Hall. Following those directions, they began walking slowly down the steps with their crowd-prods loose in their holders, but with a good-natured casualness designed to dispel any ill-feelings among the people.

It didn't work.

The guards pushed into the front ranks, shouting in voices almost inaudible to the bulk of the crowd to move on, that all gatherings had been forbidden for the immediate future, and to lodge their complaints via the more officially correct channels. The guards weren't gentle, nor were they particularly cruel—they were simply doing what they had been assigned to do. They pressed forward, and the amoebic crowd bent with the pressure, the people gathered at the contact point stepping backward into those behind them. The perimeter was moved back from the steps and then—forced by the wall of bodies behind them and the normal reaction of people hemmed into too small a space —stopped and pushed back against the guards. It became quickly and painfully obvious to those dutiful people that Vingi had overestimated the amount of co-operation they would receive, and that they should have called for disperser screens. It occurred to them that the aura of authority given them by their uniforms and guild-affiliation was a fragile thing and had deceived them into thinking themselves impervious to harm.

And then, quite suddenly, they had no time for thinking.

A guard went down (stumbled or pushed? It was a question that would remain unanswered when the incident was reviewed by the Li-Gallant) and the tone of the crowd-creature's voice changed. The timbre became deeper, more threatening. The tall man with the plant-covered neck strode through the tumult around the downed guard. He bent down, struggled against some unseen adversary, and emerged with a hand grasping a crowd-prod. He waved the instrument high, and cheers greeted his gesture of victory. Those nearest the guards, encouraged, began actively resisting. The guards pulled prods from their holders, using them liberally. Screams of genuine pain lanced the general din. The situation degenerated.

The focus of the disturbance wandered and swelled as members of various guilds found reason to fight with others. There was no single source—it was no longer even guards against the crowd, but an amalgamation of several small altercations with no definite boundaries. Combatants changed at whim.

When the edges of the riot had spread to the shield-barrier skirting Port property, the Alliance Diplos were sent out from the Center. M'Dame d'Embry had watched the fighting after being pulled from a staff meeting by a harried aide. She quickly ordered her people to stop any possible destruction of Alliance property. If the locals wanted to fight, excellent, but no Alliance holding would be harmed. The Diplo security forces used tanglefeet bombs and gas to stop the fighting and began dragging the participants away from the central melee. By the time reinforcements arrived for Vingi's harassed guards, the Diplos had settled the disturbance considerably. The Diplos withdrew back to the Center, leaving the job of caring for the wounded and arresting the appropriate number of guild-members to Vingi's more interested hands.

In time, the last remnants of the crowd had departed —walking or carted—and the area before the Hall was left to the wind, which idly toyed with scraps of paper. Bored guards, the new shift, lounged against the pillars of the Hall, staring with unfocused eyes at the birds foraging for crumbs on the steps. A few representatives, officious and hurried, nodded to the guards as they entered the doors.

All in all, just another day.

The practice room of Underasgard was a long, meandering room of the caverns, wandering crookedly and lit primarily by two parallel strips of light-emitting fungi that receded—like a badly designed painting—in a shaky v of deep perspective. The muzzy, warm light from the fungi was heavily greenish. A few hoverlamps, filtered to compensate to some degree, were distributed around the room to offset the odd coloration. A moving person walked through varying shades and tints. Racks of practice weapons lined the walls, and if the choice of weaponry seemed antiquated, it was because the Thane felt that the art of epee, foil, and saber kept the Hoorka in better physical condition, and because the proliferation of shields against most projectile and beam weapons made the blades of the romantic eras once again useful. The floor of the cavern was softer and more resilient than the hard-packed seal of the living quarters. Sound dampeners dotted the ceiling at intervals. These were the most recent addition to the room, added because the din of mock fighting echoed terrifically through the caverns and disturbed the rest of any sleeping Hoorka.

A good number of the kin could generally be found here, either practicing, watching, or gathered in the rest area at one end of the room. This day was no exception.

The Thane, Mondom, and Cranmer were standing near the central practice strip in a group of Hoorka that included Ric d'Mannberg. D'Mannberg had signed to use that strip for a long-vibro exercise. Aldhelm, who was to work with him, hadn't yet arrived.

Cranmer was carrying a camera—the tri-lensed apparatus of a portable holo. He adjusted a vernier, squinted into the eyepiece, and checked the room lighting. Somewhere inside the metal casing, a motor purred. Taking his eyes from the viewpiece, Cranmer stared critically at the lines marked on the floor of the cavern.

"Someday you're going to have to let me work against one of your apprentices," he said.

An undercurrent of laughter rippled through the Hoorka standing around him, dominated by d'Mannberg's booming chuckle. A heavy, massive man with blond-red hair and a thick beard, he looked perhaps more ponderous than dangerous. It was a deceptive appearance.

"Yah, laugh, you arrogant bastard." Cranmer turned to d'Mannberg, a comically stern frown on his face and his light tone leaching any possible sting from his words. "We scholars have our own attributes. I've a lot less flesh to move around, for one."

Stepping forward, he poked a finger into d'Mannberg's stomach. It was obvious by the sudden widening of his eyes that he was startled when his finger was repulsed by strong muscles—the gray-black folds of the Hoorka uniform were barely dented.

"You *could* always run between my legs and reach up, I suppose," d'Mannberg retorted into Cranmer's amazement. Cranmer's lack of stature led to many—too many, to Cranmer's view—comments about his shortness.

Cranmer gazed at his ineffectual forefinger, then stared appraisingly at d'Mannberg. "I doubt that it would do much good. Nothing to hold on to."

D'Mannberg winced.

"The scholar has a sting."

"At least I have *something*." As the Hoorka laughed, Cranmer shook his head, a grin on his face. "You understand," he observed at large, "it will be noted in my eventual paper that the Hoorka seem to find the crudest sort of humor appealing. Unsophisticated and rowdy, lacking taste and refinent, and indulging in gutter humor of the lowest variety. I can visualize a group of Hoorka sitting about the caverns, exchanging puns and sexual metaphors . . ."

"One must have some type of social intercourse," said Mondom, smiling overmuch.

"Sirrahs and dames, can we get our minds attuned to business?" The Thane broke in roughly. He tempered the reproof in his voice with a mock shaking of his head, but the joking conversations died. The Thane nodded toward the door leading to the Hoorka living quarters. "Aldhelm is coming."

Watching Aldhelm walk toward them, the Thane felt indecision hammering at him. The unresolved conflict of the contract night lay like a barrier between them through which only the most innocuous comments could pass, a pall of caution. *How should I speak to him? What can dissolve that curtain?* The questions remained unanswered.

As Aldhelm came up to the group of Hoorka, he acknowledged the Thane's presence with the barest salutation. "Thane, Mondom; how are you?"

As Mondom said her hello, Aldhelm glanced about and noted Cranmer's recording gear and the Hoorka waiting to see the practice bout. "An oddly popular exercise," he said drily. "Are you ready, then, Ric?"

"Definitely." D'Mannberg stretched and grunted.

Aldhelm and d'Mannberg stripped to the waist. As Aldhelm straightened and threw his tunic to the ground, the Thane caught his eye. The two locked gazes, nearly glaring, until Aldhelm shook his head with a rough motion and broke the contact. Spectators began moving away from the practice strip and the Thane felt Mondom shift position until she stood next to him. Her hand touched his thigh with a light, accidental brush held a fraction of a second too long. Suddenly sensitive to such things, the Thane could feel her warmth along his right side as he watched Cranmer film the preliminaries. He started, hesitantly, to put his arm around her shoulders, then changed his mind. He brushed his hair back.

Half-naked, Aldhelm was impressive: a wedge of a

torso with sharply defined muscles and a firm abdomen. He moved as if he were all too well aware of his physical impression, striding carefully erect and with a certain equipoise that suggested he was expecting an assault from an unseen assailant. The Thane compared it mentally with his own self—that figure he examined critically and vainly in the mirror of his room. The Thane was beginning to lose the tone and vigor of his younger days, despite his constant exercising. *No*, he thought, *in all honesty I don't exercise as I once did. I can't summon the same enthusiasm for it.* He remembered a time when he would have been eager to face the challenge of an Aldhelm, but now . . . He shook the thought away.

D'Mannberg and Aldhelm had exchanged their vibros, checking to see that each had been adjusted and locked to the practice setting. A half meter from the end of the grip to the tip, the long-vibro was a hybrid of sword and knife. Set correctly, they would sting but not cut. That was incentive enough to avoid being touched, for the welt it would leave behind was painful and slow to heal. Having checked the weapons, they returned them to each other and repeated the process: calibrate, twist the locking ring on the hilt until it clicked and moved forward, test against a fingertip—a mistake could easily cost flesh. D'Mannberg winced and shook his hand as the vibro slapped against his finger, eyes half-closed. The two Hoorka bowed to each other, and because the Thane was watching, to him. If the Thane noted that Aldhelm's bow was less deep than d'Mannberg's, he said nothing.

The combatants began to cautiously circle each other, hands outspread, bare feet hushing against the floor. As they moved, the varied color of the lights swept over them, faint washes glazing the flesh tones: green-white, then a pale purple. From another strip on the far end of the room, steel rapiers could be heard clashing with a faint ringing, but still louder was the hard breathing of Aldhelm and d'Mannberg, the low thrumming of their vibros, and the slithering of their feet on the packed earth.

D'Mannberg attacked first. A thick arm darted forward, quicker than one might have expected from the sheer mass it carried. Through a gauze of vermillion to decaying green: the vibros met with a protest of hissing rage and a few blue-white sparks that fell—a dying parabola—to the ground. Aldhelm quickly showed his superior strength. His parry combined with d'Mannberg's forward momentum to throw the larger man off-balance. D'Mannberg barely missed being nicked as he stumbled and recovered. Cranmer, filming from the side nearest them, suddenly found himself too near the combat and quickly moved backward. Laughter from the watching Hoorka pursued him. D'Mannberg, his eyes on Aldhelm, smiled ruefully in response to the amusement, thinking it directed toward his clumsy attempt to pass Aldhelm's guard. He shook his head in self-chastisement.

Aldhelm's grim expression never matched the lighthearted comments around him.

The Hoorka thrust quickly, and d'Mannberg barely had time to bring his vibro up. Their weapons shrieked agony as Aldhelm's free hand reached out and grasped d'Mannberg's vibro hand at the wrist. He twisted, viciously, and with a yelp of pain and surprise, d'Mannberg dropped his blade. Aldhlem kicked it aside as d'Mannberg shook free of Aldhelm's grip and backed away, holding the injured wrist.

(Murmured approval from the watchers. Mondom leaned close to the Thane and whispered "That was a good move. He's quick, isn't he?" The Thane grunted assent as she pressed his hand with her fingertips.)

Sweat was beginning to bead on Aldhelm's skin. On his shoulders, the fungi-lights glistened wetly. D'Mannberg, his face radiating his disgust at being so easily caught, expelled an irritated breath and reached down casually for his fallen vibro. Aldhelm, a step away, thrust at the exposed chest, and the tip of the vibro touched d'Mannberg just below the ribcage. The slap of vibro against flesh was loud in the caverns and d'Mannberg, shocked, bellowed his hurt. His fingers closed on air short of the vibro hilt; he rolled to the ground and kicked out with his legs. His left foot struck the forearm of Aldhelm's vibro arm. The weapon shivered and nearly dropped before Aldhelm could grasp it firmly again. His hand chopped at Aldhelm's leg, missing by millimeters.

"Aldhelm!" The admonishment came unbidden from the Thane, startling everyone—including himself—with its vehemence. The Hoorka-kin standing about added their own vague protest at Aldhelm's seeming disregard for practice etiquette. It was well and good to use any advantage when seriously threatened, but in practice the adversary had the right to recover a dropped weapon unless such a rule was stated beforehand. It saved people from unnecessary hurt. Aldhelm seemed too serious, too intent on showing his prowess and humbling d'Mannberg. *And it's my fault*. "Damn," said the Thane aloud.

The Thane's shout had turned Aldhelm, and in that moment d'Mannberg regained his footing. Shouting his anger, he rushed Aldhelm, getting his burly arms about the Hoorka's shoulders and bearing the smaller man down with sheer weight. On his knees, Aldhelm half-turned in d'Mannberg's hold and freed his vibro, bringing it around until it touched d'Mannberg's bicep. A yelp of pain: involuntary moisture filled d'Mannberg's eyes. He held on with desperation, but his grip had been weakened, allowing Aldhelm to turn to face him. Aldhelm lashed out with knee and vibro. His leg struck hard at d'Mannberg's thick waist, and d'Mannberg fought for breath, backing away from the threatening vibro. Sweat, rainbow-hued, rained on the floor. The hair of both men was matted to their heads, dark with moisture. D'Mannberg started forward to attack again, but his feet slid on the slick floor; in that instant, Aldhelm thrust his vibro and touched d'Mannberg's massive chest. D'Mannberg gulped for air, his eyes wide and pained. He flailed at Aldhelm, and this time struck his wrist—Aldhelm's vibro skidded across the strip. D'Mannberg struggled to rise and pursue his advantage.

A hand caught at Aldhelm's shoulder from behind as he reached for his fallen weapon, slipping once on the sweat and then gripping tightly. Aldhelm shook off the restraint with a violent motion and spun on his toes to face his new attacker—the Thane. Anger etched the lines of the older man's face even deeper. His lips were drawn back slightly from his teeth and his body was braced, the legs spread.

"Enough, Aldhelm." His voice lashed at the man. "You've managed to make your point, whatever it was supposed to be. Do you mind telling me what you're trying to prove that's worth a kin's pain?"

Aldhelm's vibro was held at his side, still activated. He stared at the Thane, a berserker rage in his eyes—dilated pupils, eyelids drawn far back. He blinked once, then again, and suddenly seemed to recognize the Hoorka ruler. His voice was almost too normal, too calm and even. "I'm a competent fighter, Thane—that's all I wished to show my kin. They needn't treat me as a nouveau or an apprentice."

"And you feel a need to demonstrate that? I'll admit it here before the rest of Hoorka, if it eases your childish temper. Or do you wish me to call a general meeting and stand up before the kin to say 'Aldhelm can fight, if he sometimes forgets to think'?" The Thane tapped a forefinger to his temple.

With the last words, Aldhelm's face moved as if struck. His hands clenched the vibro hilt convulsively.

"Let me defer to my elders then, Thane. I, the child, ask forgiveness and stand corrected. I don't think." Aldhelm spat out the words.

"Give me your vibro, then." The Thane held out his hand, and the light-fungi bathed it with an odd coloration. Glancing down, the Thane saw his palm as a dead and withered thing, devoid of power and impact, decaying and impotent. *It isn't working—this is all wrong. I should have let the others seperate them and have sent Aldhelm off to cool his temper. Just let the incident go at that with nothing said. Too late, too late. You have to play this charade out now.*

Aldhelm glanced at the Thane's hand. "The vibro?" he asked. And he stared at the Thane in mute challenge, making no move to hand over the weapon.

Anger fought logic inside the Thane, anger allied with a need to prove his own competence to himself and sweep away the doubts that had come to bother him more of late. He glanced at Aldhelm, at the vibro, at the muscular body confronting him. It would be easy to simply stand there, hand out; Aldhelm would give in from the force of the Hoorka-kin watching at the Thane's back. The younger Hoorka was in the wrong and knew it—and it would be a strengthening of the Thane's authority. All he need do was wait.

But he couldn't wait.

Without a word, the Thane pulled his tunic over his head as a small, rational part of his mind shrilled alarm. He held the bunched cloth in his hand, then threw it at Aldhelm and leaped to follow. He heard Mondom's voice crying wordlessly as he struck out at the man.

The Thane's attack knocked Aldhelm to the ground, the Hoorka still trying to free himself from the tunic. They fell in a tangle of limbs, the Thane with both hands on Aldhelm's knife arm. Aldhelm thrust the blinding cloth aside and levered himself with his powerful legs, driving and turning so that the Thane found himself below the other man, still holding desperately to the vibro hand.

By the Hag, he's strong. I've made a mistake. I can't take him. The realization came even as he brought his knees up in a reflex motion, searching for groin or stomach. But Aldhelm had anticipated that maneuver and had moved quickly to the left, his body braced against the pressure of the Thane's grip. The Thane let go his hold of Aldhelm. The sudden loss of support toppled Aldhelm. The Thane brought interlocked hands down between the man's shoulderblades and scrambled to his feet.

Too low. I hit him too low and too late.

Aldhelm regained his footing almost as quickly, but Mondom and another of the Hoorka took him by the arms before he could move to attack the Thane once more. He glowered angrily, but didn't struggle.

"Let him go. Let him try to finish it." The Thane was breathing heavily, feeling weaker than he should for the amount of exertion. His mind still shouted its admonition, but the adrenalin—the excitement of the fight—had taken him. He felt he had to carry through this farce or face an unresolved problem. *But if you lose . . . No, I won't lose.* He nodded at Aldhelm. "You wanted this, kin. Let him go, Mondom."

"Thane—"

"Let him go!" The voice was like the slap of a whip on flesh. She released Aldhelm. The Thane stooped and picked up d'Mannberg's vibro from the floor of the strip and checked the setting. "Come on then, Hoorka."

Aldhelm didn't move. The rage had gone from him, and his eyes searched the Thane. "You don't have to do this. You'll lose, Thane, and it will prove nothing." His voice was suddenly soft and penitent. "What do you demand of me? My apology to Ric? He has it." Aldhelm nodded to d'Mannberg. "My vibro? Here."

Aldhelm held his weapon out to the Thane, hilt foremost.

The cavern was silent, the Hoorka watching. Mondom stirred, her voice low and pleading.

"Thane, take it."

"No!" He shouted the word. *I can't. Don't you see that?* "You wished to practice, Aldhelm. I need the exercise myself. Defend yourself, Hoorka."

They came together in the middle of the strip. Their hands locked, the vibros clashed once, then twice more before Aldhelm, grunting with the effort, threw the Thane back. The Thane stumbled, his ankle turning beneath him, and he swung his hands wide in an attempt to maintain equilibrium. Aldhelm did not hesitate to take the opening. He came at the Thane as the older man strove to recover his balance. The Thane brought his vibro up a fraction of a second too late: in a flurry of sparks, he turned the blade, but the searing hiss of the vibro tip marked his side. He grimaced in pain as he parried and prepared to meet another thrust, but Aldhelm had moved back, waiting.

The Thane, his side aflame, saw that the Hoorka was holding his vibro too low and he thrust at the opening, coming in over Aldhelm's blade. He met flesh, and saw with satisfaction a red welt form high on Aldhelm's shoulder. He continued his attack, following his advantage as the excitement flowed more swiftly in his veins. His body seemed to have shed some of its years, shed even the weariness of a minute before. He thought, oddly at variance with his earlier pessimism, that he might have a chance. Aldhelm, yes, was stronger; still, experience . . .

Aldhelm backed and parried, the Thane following eagerly. Near the back line of the practice strip, Aldhelm kicked out with a foot, almost sending the Thane to the ground as his heel brushed the Thane's knee. Now it was the Thane who retreated as they circled, feinting and jabbing without making contact. The cavern floor was becoming slippery with their sweat, the footing uncertain and treacherous. A drop of perspiration burned its way into the Thane's left eye. He blinked it away. At the edge of his vision, he could see Cranmer filming, with Mondom beside him, her face showing her concern.

Old man, old man, hurry this farce. The Thane's breathing was harsh and too quick, accompanied by a thin wheezing. He knew he must make a final move, win or lose, very soon. The euphoria had been false, the adrenalin weak. His body would all too soon succumb to the punishment.

Aldhelm thrust again, coming at the Thane with his arm extended. In deflecting the blade, the Thane felt a searing pull at his side where he'd been touched by Aldhelm's vibro, and knew that he could not retain his mobility much longer. Time would award Aldhelm victory. The Thane judged his distance, waited for the slightest relaxation in Aldhelm's defense. When he thought he saw the opening, he attacked.

Vibros snapped and snarled, clattering against each other. The Thane drove his other hand, fisted, toward Aldhelm's stomach as the younger Hoorka tried to twist away, his eyes wide with the vehemence of the Thane's attack. But the Thane's fist found its mark, though the blow was partially deflected by an instinctive shielding by Aldhelm's forearm. Aldhelm fought for breath, pushing back against the Thane as their vibros slid—with an aching, high-frequency squeal—along each other's lengths. The Thane felt more than saw the blades disengage. Too close to Aldhelm, he moved to parry the expected riposte. He found nothing.

Again Aldhelm's vibro burned him, this time slapping at the skin over his heart. He screamed in inarticulate agony as Aldhelm's open hand drove into his chin, thrusting him backward. The Thane fought for balance, arms flailing, and fell with one leg underneath him. He broke the fall with his elbows, but the breath was knocked from him. Aldhelm flicked off his vibro as the Thane struggled to breathe.

Aldhelm stared at the Thane with an unreadable emotion on his face. His mouth worked and he started to speak; he suddenly shook his head and threw his vibro to the ground away from the Thane. Limping slightly, a hand kneading his bruised shoulder, he turned from the Thane and walked away.

Seven

A single smear of light.

Cranmer rubbed his hands over his eyes to clear them, not sure of what it was that he saw in the darkness before him. The rubbing only produced the blindness of retinal colors—a pulsing orange blob that slowly went purple. It was several moments before it faded and his eyes re-adjusted to the darkness. He peered into the cavern-night ahead of him as if trying to pierce a thick fog. His thumb fidgeted over the switch to his hoverlamps but he kept them unlit, waiting in the dark of Underasgard.

Yes, it was still there.

There were shifting colors—gold to yellow green like the liquid shades of a late afternoon sun in summer, a light that was pierced by bars of black that seemed to enclose it. To one side was a darker silhouette like an irregular hill. It took a moment for Cranmer to synthesize the asbtractness of the scene, and then it all fell into perspective. The light, a hoverlamp set on the ground; the bars, the skeleton of the ippicator; the hill, the hunched shoulder of the Thane covered with his nightcloak. The hoverlamp must have been set inside the body of the ippicator, oscillating slightly and giving out only a dim illumination, for the light died before reaching the walls of the cavern. Cranmer hesitated and started to turn back, not wanting to disturb the Thane's obvious meditation. In turning, his shoe scraped rock loudly, and the black shape of the Thane moved and rose.

"Thane?" Cranmer called out, resigning himself, and hoping that a knife was not on its way.

Shadows raced over rock as the hoverlamp inside the ippicator flared into sudden brilliance, striping the distant roof with the distorted image of the skeleton.

"Cranmer? Damnit, man, identify yourself when you sneak up behind a person."

"Yah. You want a companion? If you don't care for company, sirrah, simply say so. I could always pretend I was looking for the kitchens and got lost."

The Thane shrugged, not seeming to take notice of Cranmer's attempt at levity. Cranmer took the shrug for assent. He switched on his lamps and moved over the broken ground toward the ippicator.

The Thane said nothing as the scholar approached. His eyes were fixed on the hoverlamp inside the skeleton, a shadow from the ribs across his eyes like a mask. Cranmer, amidst the noise of disturbed pebbles, came up to stand next to him. He stood there, shielding his eyes from the glare and glancing from the Hoorka to the ippicator. The Thane touched the control belt and the light dimmed once more and began to oscillate, like a caged, golden fire.

"It's cold here." Cranmer could think of no other overture to conversation, and he was sure it sounded as inane to the Thane as it did to his own ears. The Hoorka was obviously disconsolate and moody—it seemed part of the introspective man's nature, but Cranmer had never seen it so naked, without any attempt to mask the melancholia. Cranmer, after waiting what seemed an appropriate time for a reply to his comment and receiving none, sat on the stones next to the Thane. He could feel the chill of the rock through his clothing.

Cranmer made another attempt at conversation. "You know, after you showed me this skeleton, I went back to my rooms and checked with my data-link to Center. Seems the latest theory in favor states that the ippicator became extinct not before, but during the Settling. The Neweden Archives are in such poor shape that it can't be verified—the Interregnum did that to the records of a hundred worlds, I know . . . But evidently the ippicators couldn't compete with us or adapt well enough to survive. They had to be dying out long before the Settling, but there were reports of ippicator sightings in some of the wilder regions. I don't know . . . You would think that some of the Settlers would have made some effort to save the beast, if only for its physical appearance, if the theory is true."

The Thane grunted a monosyllabic reply.

Silence. The lamp flickered inside the ippicator.

"Mondom received a new contract," Cranmer said.

Now the Thane moved. He seemed to note Cranmer for the first time. His head turned and dark eyes moved under the shadow of his brow. He stirred, stretching slightly. "She knows what to do with it," he said finally. "You didn't come back here just to tell me that." His voice was a challenge, a question.

"No. When I noticed you'd gone, I thought it'd be easier to speak with you back here, away from Hoorka-kin." Cranmer paused and the Thane looked back at the ippicator.

"Speak, then," he said, gruffly.

"You're probably not going to be pleased."

A shrug. "I'm not pleased with much at the moment."

"Anything I say is said as an outsider, I know. To the Hoorka-kin, I'm a lassari and an offworlder, but I *do* have an interest in and a liking for Hoorka. I don't want to see the kin destroyed any more than you would, and not simply for selfish reasons. Hoorka could die now, at this moment, and I'd simply incorporate that extinction into my eventual work. It wouldn't alter the interest in it that the academic community would have. But I wouldn't want to see that. Truly."

"Why do scholars have such a burning need to preamble their statements to death?"

"Because you don't seem to be taking criticism very well, and I want you to understand why I speak." Cranmer spoke sharply, mild irritation in his voice that awakened echoes in the rocks. He softened his voice. "Thane, I know I've no right to speak, which is why I'm being so circumspect, but I thought you'd be better able to listen to me than your kin. Quite simply and brutally, Thane, you've been stupid. You don't seem to think of yourself as guild-elder of the Hoorka, and what alarms me most is that you don't seem to care a great deal. Your decisions of late have been at best mediocre. You're putting crises aside rather than dealing with them."

Cranmer looked at the Thane's face, searching for a reaction.

Nothing.

"Your handling of Aldhelm . . ." Cranmer shook his head, his hands cupping air. "You didn't do much to dispel anyone's uneasiness. Even if you'd beaten him, what good would it have done? I don't pretend to understand the subtleties of Neweden kinship, but even this violent world can't believe that a physical victory symbolizes the truth of intellectual assertions. Or do you think it does? What are you thinking?"

"My thoughts are my own." Curtly, without a glance.

"But your actions are Hoorka's. Do you remember that? Or do you just sit here feeling sorry for yourself?"

Now the Thane glared angrily at the smaller man, who looked back with a calmness he didn't feel. Then the Thane twisted his head away with a savage motion, his eyes intent once again on the ippicator. "I made Hoorka into the guild-kin it is. My father was lassari when he came here, but *I* made myself a niche in this society. My actions *should* be Hoorka's. Do you dispute that?"

"Yah, to a degree." Cranmer, feeling the heat of the Thane's gaze, hastened to explain. "I've told you my thoughts before. I don't say you should step down—though if this continues, that might well be my counsel. I suggest instead that you do something and quickly. Act more decisively. You endanger what you've built: you might bring it down with you, destroy all you've strived for."

"Is that the extent of your advice?"

Cranmer lifted one shoulder and let it fall. "I suppose."

"It's easy to see flaws, no matter how beautiful the gem that encloses them. Can you tell me how to cut and polish this stone to remove all the imperfections?"

"I can point out those imperfections as you work, and that's to your advantage. I suppose you know that your little fight with Aldhelm was a grave mistake."

The last words seemed to finally kindle the building wrath inside the Thane. With a whispering of cloth, the

Hoorka leapt to his feet, the nightcloak swirling. Cranmer threw up his hands in instinctive defense.

"I don't *need* your advice," the Thane shouted, the words ringing in the cavern. "I don't care for your manufactured guilt, either. I can furnish enough of my own." And with a much-practiced motion, he drew and activated his vibro. Its humming filled Cranmer's ears. The Thane's arm drew back, poised for an instant, and then he threw the blade. It sped true.

With an arid crack, the vibro severed a rib from the ippicator's shoulder and lodged itself deeply in the animal's spine. The vibro's low hum died as dust settled to earth.

Cranmer found himself lying on his side, arms hugging himself. He sat up slowly, his breath loud and quick.

The Thane's shadow was huge on the cavern wall behind him as he stood, his hands at his side, his head down, the feet slightly spread. The Hoorka raised his head as with an effort, glancing at the weapon impaling the dead beast.

"You've said nothing I haven't thought myself, Cranmer." He strode over to the ippicator and pulled on the hilt of the vibro. It came loose easily. The Thane held the weapon in his hand for a moment, staring at the broken rib on the cavern floor. He put it back in its scabbard.

"Did I frighten you, scholar?" The Thane came over and sat next to Cranmer. His voice had an odd jocularity. "Good. I scare myself. I've done so many dumb things of late."

The Thane allowed a slight smile to lift the corners of his mouth. "And I become rather too maudlin and melodramatic, also," he continued. "No, I don't need your advice, my friend—I've counseled myself with the same words you've used, and perhaps more harshly than you might suspect."

"Have you thought of resigning as active head?"

For a moment, the anger returned to the Thane's face, creasing the forehead and inflaming the broken veins of his cheeks. Then it died, as quickly as it had come, as if there were no longer any internal fuel on which it could feed. "Yes," he answered. "But events are moving. The Hoorka are involved in a crisis that I can see forming, and I can't bring myself to trust anyone else. Aldhelm—yes, he's a leader and the kin would probably follow him if I gave them leave to do so, but he needs tempering or he'll break under the pressures. He's too quick to make his choices and he tends to see things in some two-value logic of his own devising; no shades or degrees, just Right and Wrong. And Mondom—I'm afraid that I diffused her effectiveness by being her lover. The kin might think I've named her as my successor only because of my affection for her. Sartas—he's far too headstrong, too argumentative, and not all that well-liked. And myself . . ." He put his hands out, palms upward. Cranmer saw callouses there. "I suppose I have my own problems," the Thane said, "but *I made Hoorka*. It's my onus, my responsibility, and I need to make the decisions. If I fail, at least I can only blame myself for that failure."

"It adds unneccesary burdens to your mind. What of your gods? Can't you find consolation there, some guidance in your teachings?"

"Did you see priests at the ceremony, scholar?" The Thane smiled, almost sadly. "As head of the kin, I am the mediator between Hoorka and the gods. Whom can I go to when the gods don't answer? And I suspect that you are not a religious man, Cranmer. Do you think gods would interfere and guide my path?"

"No."

"And neither do I." The Thane spoke slowly, quietly. "Hoorka faces a challenge. I intend to see us through it. Afterwards, perhaps I'll consider your words and my own doubts."

"Now you sound sure of yourself once more."

The Thane shook his head. He looked at Cranmer with pained eyes. "I wish I were. I feel no different."

The Thane touched his belt and the lamp inside the ippicator died completely, the golden fire fading into the eternal night of Underasgard. The two men sat there for a time, listening to the silence around them.

Gunnar toyed with a Tarot deck, thumbing through the dog-eared and brilliantly-colored pieces of pasteboard. It was an old set, stained with use—most of which was not his

—and not even holographic. The pictures stared back flatly, inked on the surface of the cards. He'd once had the deck appraised by a dealer in oddities at Sterka Port—the woman had found it to be worth more than he'd anticipated: the deck was over two centuries old, and from Terra itself. To maintain their value and their use (the Knight of Swords had once been folded in half and was in danger of tearing), he knew he should avoid handling them often or carrying them about; it wasn't advice he often followed.

The cards gave him pleasure, and he liked to imagine that he could feel an undercurrent of power in them. Gunnar wasn't so self-deceiving as to imagine that he could tap that power, but somewhere back in the deck's murky history a person of sensitivity had possessed them, and it pleased Gunnar to believe that he could detect the residue of that power hidden in the cards.

Gunnar held a card up to the sunlight that lanced across the room like a palpable shaft until it struck the far wall and was broken. Too-saturated colors just beginning to fade: they glistened and awakened in the light, the gilt and silver shimmering. Potok, from across the room, could see a little of the card's face—an old man sitting on an ornate throne, the arms of which ended in carved ram's heads. The man held an ankh-sceptre in one hand and a globe in the other with a bleary and desolate mountain range hunched in the background under a lowering sky lanced by rays from a hidden star.

"A pretty card, neh?" said Gunnar. He flipped it around in the sunlight, enjoying the way reflections shot from the slick surface. He let the card slide to the desk at which he was seated, watching it fall with one hand cupping his chin. It landed face up.

"The Emperor," he said, "a card of leadership and temporal power, of logic besting emotion. Considering the time in which these cards were evidently manufactured, I've wondered if the old man isn't supposed to be the tyrant Huard. He looks like the old bastard, doesn't he?"

Gunnar picked up the card and shuffled it back into the deck. He stacked the cards carefully, then began laying them out in the Celtic mode, mumbling under his breath.

"I almost think you believe in those things." Potok

moved forward. His figure—in robes of Assembly blue—eclipsed the window light, so that the room darkened with a premature twilight. Lamps throughout the room kindled themselves to compensate for the reduced illumination.

"They're here," said Gunnar. "How can I not believe in them?"

"You know what I meant."

Gunnar smiled. "At times, I almost find myself wanting to believe in a foreplanned future. That can be a comforting notion, knowing that the gods have set out everything beforehand. And the Hoorka, like our own guild, profess a belief in Dame Fate. Why couldn't there be a device in which we could see Her intent?"

"The Hoorka." Potok harrumphed. "You're so certain those Tarot can foretell the future?"

"The Tarot don't predict. They indicate possibilities. That's a subtle difference, kin-brother." One hand toyed with the cards, idly riffling the wear-softened edges. "They can suggest what will occur should all things remain the same. You can change the fortune if you heed their advice."

"Whatever." Potok waved an impatient hand.

"That's your trouble, Potok. You're too impatient."

Potok shrugged, his face revealing a mild irritation. "And what do you and your cards suggest for our future course of action?"

"I assume by that you mean what are we going to do with our dear Li-Gallant?"

"I do."

"I don't know." Again Gunnar smiled. "Haven't thought about it all that much, to be truthful." He leaned back in his chair and clasped his hands behind his head. "You are sure, then, that it was Vingi's contract that the Hoorka were working?"

"Who else would want you dead so badly? Have you insulted anyone other than him? And who else would be so cowardly not to declare bloodfeud and settle it face to face? Yes, I'm sure it was Vingi." Potok folded his arms across his chest. About him, dust-motes swirled in the sun. He stood in a field of golden pollen.

Gunnar chuckled at the image—had it been a muscular

young person standing in the yellow warmth with righteou anger on his face, perhaps it wouldn't have seemed humorous. But it was Potok, short and pudgy. Gunnar laughed, and Potok's face took on an aspect of puzzlement.

"Sit down, man," said Gunnar, waving a hand toward a nearby floater. "You look too pompous standing there. Sit down. Let's not fool ourselves, my kin. My guild-kin were frightened enough of Vingi when the contract came—no one offered to come with me to protect me from Hoorka weapons. Your anger is odd in light of that."

Potok said nothing. He looked at Gunnar's smile, which no longer was a gesture of humor, but a deadly thing, sharp and menacing. Potok sat back in his floater, pursed his lips, then sat up abruptly once more.

"Gunnar, the Li-Gallant is confused. He half-believes that we've somehow managed to bribe the Hoorka to our side—at least this is what my sources in his guild tell me. Despite Vingi's protestations to the contrary, the Hoorka would give Neweden security forces a problem. So Vingi's poised, ready to move either way but afraid to commit himself. He'd drag both our guild and the Hoorka into an Assembly trial and have us disbanded if he thought he could make his charges stand. We can use his doubts."

Gunnar nodded. "By using the Hoorka."

"By using their reputation. We might be able to force their hand."

Gunnar shook his head. "I don't know. The basic idea is appealing, but I don't know." His fingertips brushed the Tarot deck idly.

Potok leaned forward and reached out as if to pick up the cards, but Gunnar placed his hand over them. "If you don't mind," he said. "Superstition"—with a slight laugh—"says that no one else is supposed to handle your Tarot unless he's the subject of a reading."

"Give me a reading, then. For that matter, read your own fate and ease your doubts. We should grasp this situation while Vingi waits."

"You're sure it's necessary to approach the Hoorka?" Gunnar shivered, despite the sunlit warmth of the room. The Hoorka reputation exceeded the truth—their portrait was one of bloodthirsty killers happy only when in the act of slaughter threatrically macabre—but it was a truth that no guild enjoyed doing business with the assassins. And no guild had yet dared to risk bloodfeud with them. Gunnar didn't wish his own guild to be the one to perform that experiment. "It could be dangerous, Potok. Let me ask you, have you kept an edge on your fencing skills?"

"The Hoorka can't get involved in vendettas against other guilds. It would destroy them. They're safe."

"Tell me that after they've chased *you*." Gunnar looked at Potok, who found the scene outside the window suddenly interesting. "Would a vendetta destroy the Hoorka? And would you care to take that chance, knowing that the result might be that you nestle in Hag Death's arms earlier than you wish?"

Potok glanced at the Tarot, then at Gunnar. "I'm here suggesting it, kin-brother."

"It might destroy the guild." Gunnar hesitated. "Brother," he added.

"I don't think so."

"It might destroy Hoorka."

"You'd care?"

Gunnar laughed. "Not at all." He began spreading out the cards. "Not at all," he repeated. "In fact, I might well enjoy that more than thwarting Vingi."

Gunnar plucked a card at random from the deck and turned it face up on the desk. On the painted surface, a horse strode, bearing a skeleton dressed in ancient armour and bearing a tattered banner. Below the apparition, people prostrated themselves. The skeleton grinned as the horse trampled them underneath.

The Li-Gallant Vingi was wearing a loose tunic and pants, all woven of a soft, bluish material showing the thinness of much use. Vingi wore this when he desired comfort rather than ostentation; in private, that was often. It was a uniform most of the guild-kin that formed his private staff saw often and were used to, but it tended to startle those whose image of the Li-Gallant was the public one.

The Domoraj, though head of the security force of Vingi's guild, was not one of the privileged few.

The Domoraj stared more than would be considered

polite by the standards of kinship, taking in the frayed sleeves, the worn elbows, the stains that had gotten past the dirtshield and set in the fabric—a mustard-brown splotch putting a tentative pseudopod on Vingi's breast fascinated him. The Domoraj forced his eyes up past the clothing to the corpulent face. He set his lips, hoping that the Li-Gallant had missed his insubordination.

Vingi, however, was engrossed in a com-unit set on his desk and in an iced drink that resided—glass sides sweating—in one hand. The sea-green light of the com-unit washed over his face from below, giving his features an unnatural edging. Vingi sipped once at his drink, nodded thoughtfully at the screen, and flicked the unit's controls. The light slowly receded and Vingi's large, almost sorrowful eyes found the Domoraj.

"I just had a less than satisfactory report, sirrah," he said without preliminary. "It appears that Gunnar has gained some popularity since his escape from the Hoorka. Two previously unaligned guilds have given their Assembly votes to Gunnar's kin. The Weaver's Guild of Tellis has rescinded their support of our guild and will send a representative to the Assembly until they make a decision on which ruling guild will represent them. What does that suggest to you?"

The Domoraj shifted his position in his seat. Vingi's sudden gaze bothered him—he was too used to the deference of the guild-kin under him.

"I'm a military man," he said. "I have no part in the governing affairs of our kin, Li-Gallant. And I don't pretend to meddle in politics. I take my orders from you, sirrah. That's sufficient." It was temporizing, but he could think of nothing else to say.

Vingi shook his head. "No, kin-brother, that won't do. Every person living on Neweden dabbles in politics. It's impossible not to take a stand unless one is lassari. There are no neutral guilds."

"There are the Hoorka."

"Yah, the Hoorka." Vingi sat his drink down on his desk and shook moisture from his hand. "The Hoorka," he repeated. "What do you think of them, Domoraj? As a, ahh, 'military man'?"

"In what respect, Li-Gallant? They're excellently trained and very good at what they do . . ." He shrugged.

Vingi lifted an arm and plucked a loose thread from the sleeve of his tunic. For a few moments his attention was completely on that small task and he ignored the other man. Finally, he looked up again.

"A pity things must eventually wear out—and it is always the favorites. But"—he changed the topic with an inflection—"I meant, do you think the Hoorka as apolitical as they claim to be? Yah, they have no voice in the Assembly and stay prominently distant from the constant bloodfeuds of the guilds, but does that prove their neutrality in the affairs of Neweden?"

"I don't know." Simply.

Vingi nodded. He sighed. "*That* was not the answer I desired. Let me phrase it this way: Do you find it odd that Gunnar managed to escape?"

"I see your point, Li-Gallant." The Domoraj was carefully neutral, his hands folded on his lap, his back stiff and not touching the back of his chair: a man as careful as his appearance. When he killed, he killed daintily, he killed with finesse and affected grace. "Victims *have* escaped the Hoorka before," he said. "It's essential to their existence —and at the risk of incurring your wrath, kin-brother, the men I sent—at *your* behest—to insure Gunnar's death did no better."

Vingi's face was briefly touched by anger. It trembled his chin. "And they were very clumsy to have killed m'Dame Cuscratti. You needn't remind me of such things. My point, however, is that none that have previously escaped the assassins have been so important or influential."

"The gods sometimes do smile on odd people." The Domoraj was also devout—it was a matter of some humor among his subordinates that the Domoraj spent as much time praying to the gods as sending others to their domain.

"Don't speak of Dame Fate's whims."

The Domoraj, unsure of his ground or perhaps simply shocked by the hint of blasphemy in his leader, waited in silence.

Vingi idly rubbed a forefinger over the lip of his glass. Outside his office, the two men could hear the hushing of a soft tread as a watchroboi passed along the hallway. Vingi leaned forward. "You have contacts, Domoraj. I want Gunnar killed, but I don't want to tie up our guild's resources with a formal bloodfeud."

"Is that wise, Li-Gallant? The other guilds—"

"—will not find out," the Li-Gallant finished. "Don't spout ethics to me, Domoraj. Dame Fate smiles on those who grasp their own lives. Find me a lassari that's competent enough to do the task. Then do a hypnofix on him so that he thinks he's acting of his own volition and can't be traced back to us if he should fail. That should suffice."

The Domoraj said nothing.

Vingi leaned back and took up his drink once more. "I'm not a person given to subtle tactics," he said. "It's been said that my bluntness indicates a lack of my kin-father's skill with such things. No"—he raised a hand as the Domoraj began the obligatory objection—"you needn't say anything. I have my ears, my sources of information. I might even be tempted to acknowledge it as a partial truth. Still, I see a simple solution, one that fits Neweden. If Gunnar falls to a lassari, the guilds will withdraw their support of his guild—a man with kin that would fall to a lassari. Yah, that would indeed suffice. The guilds won't think Gunnar's organization strong enough, no matter who heads the guild."

The Domoraj watched as Vingi switched his com—unit on. The tide of sea-light rushed over him noiselessly. Vingi waved an impatient hand in dismissal.

"You have a task, guild-brother. See to it, and may Dame Fate guide your choice."

Eight

A triangle of milky light slashed across the viewscreen set in m'Dame d'Embry's desk. The light trailed across the front of the desk and across the grassed floor to a genesis at the window. There, the Neweden sun (she could never fall into the habit of referring to it in the Neweden way as the 'sunstar') glowered down at a new day. The glare made it difficult for her to see the screen; she moved so that her thin body blocked the distracting light. Her hand passed over a contact. The screen responded with an inner illumination of its own, caught in which were the head and shoulders of her secretary.

"Karl," she said immediately, "I want to speak to the Hoorka-thane. When you reach him, I'll take the call here." She switched off his "Yes, m'Dame," leaning back in her chair and allowing her body a moment of relaxation. She was all too aware of the fact that she seemed to need more of these interludes each standard. *Tired, getting old,* she thought. *Old.* Yet she still managed to retain her reputation as perhaps the most successful liaison for the Diplomatic Resource Team—the Diplos—*and* as the most crusty of them. She could remember all the forgotten, misplaced and unwanted worlds she'd cajoled into some semblance of normalcy within the Alliance; picking up the shards of Huard's empire and the age of sundering that followed the tyrant's death. . . .

She shook her head. *Daydreaming again.* She rebuked

herself inwardly. Waiting for the call from the Thane, she let her eyes wander about the office.

She allowed herself few luxuries. A holo of a d'Vellia soundsculpture always seemed to be present in her offices (the more persistent rumors among the staffers were that she had once had an affair with that temperamental sculptor), and an animo-painting by some anonymous artist went through random changes on the wall, a last remnant of a fad that had been popular many standards back. The only touch of richness was an etched ippicator bone—the ankle of the fifth leg, she would point out to curious visitors—which was a gift from the Li-Gallant Vingi. It was, perhaps, worth more than anything else in the room, a rare item that offworld collectors would pay much to acquire. Other than these, the room was unornamented. Even the viewscreen on the desk echoed the room—the lowest Diplo staffer had a holo comlink rather than a flat viewscreen. With reverse snobbery, d'Embry prided herself on her austerity.

Her reverie was broken by a sprinkling of lightning across the desk. On the viewscreen, random dots, prodded and cajoled, formed themselves into Karl's face.

"M'Dame, I have the Thane."

"I'm ready to speak with him, then." She leaned back in her chair. "and bring me a pot of tea when I've finished, please. Thank you, Karl."

"Yah, m'Dame." The screen dimmed and motes of bluish white danced a hesitant ballet before giving way to the image of the Hoorka-thane. His lips moved, the last sparks of interference flitting across his scarred cheeks.

"M'Dame d'Embry." The Thane nodded. Beyond him, d'Embry could see stone walls and an apprentice Hoorka working on some indiscernible task, hunched over a bench. The complaining whine of a drill rasped the speaker.

"I'll be brief, Thane. Quite simply, there have been allegations passing through Sterka—rumors—that concern me. Most of them revolve around you and your organization's relationships with the, ahh, political aspirants, shall we say, of the Neweden Assembly."

As she spoke, she watched the face in the screen. The deep-set eyes narrowed, the lips set themselves in a thin line, a new ridge formed in the forehead as if he were holding back . . . anger? irritation? Well, he could indulge in temper if he wished. "The Li-Gallant," she continued, "has asked me to withdraw my consideration of letting your guild operate offworld. He's also mentioned bringing the Hoorka forward in the Assembly."

D'Embry's hand reached out and found the smooth surface of the ippicator bone, the thin valleys of the carved lines. "Between the two of us, Thane, I don't think you need to concern yourself greatly with that latter threat. As I understand your people's odd social structure, he can't afford to invoke the wrath of Gunnar's guild in a bloodfeud. He'd lose face—or worse—unless conditions were ripe for such actions. But he *is* insistent, and he *is* the head of local government. I have told the Li-Gallant"—with the proper amount of emphasis on the word "told"—"that I will hold a brief, very informal meeting here at the Center in two local days."

Through this, the Thane had looked increasingly impatient, though he did not interrupt. He glanced frequently to one side of the screen, as if his interest lay elsewhere. "Is that an invitation for me to attend, m'Dame?"

For once, d'Embry found a disadvantage in simplicity. There were overtones in his resonant voice that were lost in the reproduction of the viewer, nuances that she wanted to read. Was he simply being offhandedly sarcastic or humorously flippant? No, not the last. The Thane didn't seem to be a man with humor: a dry, worn-out husk of a man. Had he ever laughed? she wondered.

"I hope you'll be there, Thane. The Li-Gallant and Potok will also attend. I frankly consider the entire business a waste of my time and I don't have a great deal of that commodity to squander, if you'll pardon my bluntness. But I *am* the Alliance Regent for Neweden"—she paused—"and the Li-Gallant did insist. I have neither the inclination nor the staff to undertake an investigation of the whole situation, and my people don't have enough feel for your guild-kinship structure to judge you fairly. Therefore I need the interested parties to outline their stands."

"Hoorka has no stance."

No, definitely no humor to him at all. He is, instead, quite comically serious.

"Even neutrality is a stance, Thane. And as I understand the guilds, only lassari can have true neutrality. A person with kin must be loyal to his kin. That is a stance."

The shoulders in the viewscreen rose in a minor shrug. "Is that all you wished to say, m'Dame?" In the voice of a hurried man, with the implication of a task waiting.

"You'll be here?"

"I will, if it serves Hoorka."

"Then that is all I need to say, Thane. Good day, sirrah."

The contact was broken, and before she could gather her thoughts to fit them into her impression of the Thane, the door dilated and Karl brought in a tray.

"Your tea, m'Dame?"

Its bittersweet aroma filled the room.

Night.

Violet scarves of clouds wrapped two spheres, one large and saffron and caught in the dark fingers of trees; the other smaller and cold, becalmed at zenith: Sleipnir and Gulltopp. Double shadows—one purple-tinged—clawed at the earth. It was quiet and watchfully peaceful, the landscape.

A distraction in the scene: a figure moved. It shushed aside scattered leaves of the nearly-spent autumn. A light-shunter moved patterns of elusive dark across his/her clothing and moonlight stuttered across shapes at its waist as it moved through knee-level grasses toward the house on the knoll. With the laughter of dry leaves, the wind flung clouds to the horizon and freed the moons. In the instant before the light-shunter reacted to the increased light and fuzzed the figure's outlines again, it could be seen more clearly.

She was a tall, almost emaciated woman. Her startled eyes looked upward at the sky's betrayal.

Near the interface of meadow grass and stately lawn, she paused. She looked up toward the house and the trees gathered at the crest of the hill, all dark against the moonlit sky. There were no signs of life or vigilance.

Good. This might be easier, then.

The windows of the house were polarized black, or the rooms beyond them were dark: she could not tell which. Either way, no one could easily see her. She went to her knees in the tall grass, checking the equipment hung on her belt. No signs of life, but already a detector was flashing its awareness of a warning field just ahead. She fumbled at a loop and unhooked a cylinder of black metal rimmed with switches. She flipped one, then another, watching a red light on the detector with intense eyes. It pulsed red, then an amber that burned and slowly died. She smiled into darkness, patted the cylinder, and replaced it at her side. She rose again to her feet.

The transition to lawn was more heard than seen—the light-shunter fogged her perception of the scene—as the tidal soughing of weeds gave way to the soft padding of low grass. She could feel her pants, wet from mid-thigh to ankle, clinging to her legs with cold dampness. But treated fabrics that resisted moisture also tended to be noisier when moving. A small thing, but it would be small things that kept her alive tonight.

She began to curve diagonally up the hill toward the side of the house, remembering the whispered advice given to her the night before in a Port bar near the Center. Her contact had taken her over toward the bio-pilot's alcove, away from the general commotion of the place. He had detailed the grounds and obstacles she might expect to meet; the entrances to the home and how they might be guarded. The information, if correct, was invaluable. If wrong . . . it meant little. She hated Gunnar, who had once refused her membership in his guild. She hated all he stood for, and if her contact knew of someone that would pay her to do this, all the better. The payment had been generous, at least the half she'd managed to get in advance. Last night had been more than pleasant. The euphoria still clung to her, diaphanous.

They'd gone together to his rooms, and she'd slept for a while. Yes, and she'd woken with a fierce passion against Gunnar. It remained, a backdrop, to the more gentle passions she felt that night.

She was aware of trouble before she could physically

sense it. A momentary prickling shivered along her back. She crouched, rolled, and sought cover without thinking . . . but there was no cover on that hillside.

She heard, suddenly, the electric crackling of a sting, and her right side tingled with the near miss—she'd been seen. She felt the beginning of panic. A scream rose in her throat, and she forced it down.

Her contact had told her—in his harsh, sibilant whisper—that Gunnar's house was not well-guarded, that she would have no trouble once past the shield. She'd been skeptical, even then, but the money he had shown her and the things the money had bought . . .

She rolled again, the opposite way, as she freed a hand laser from its holster and fired toward the house. She knew she had next to no chance of hitting someone, but hoped it would confuse the person with the sting long enough for her to run to the meadow grass and the small protection it would bring. Gunnar. She hated him and his guild all the more, and she felt keen frustration at being thwarted. The wash of emotion blunted the first onrushing of panic. She began to think again. She raked laser fire across the darkened front of the house, smelling the acrid fumes of burning paint.

There had been, first, the Stretcher: an innocuous-looking pill that had elongated her time sense. It had taken a week to yawn, a hour to raise glass to lips . . .

The sting barked again, and again it struck very near her. She abandoned stealth and ran.

. . . and the girl who'd been so co-operative once her palm had been crossed with silver. Her hands had been slick and smooth like malleable porcelain, her breasts small and girlish . . .

She switched direction at random, with little hope. The moons were bright, the light-shunter was poor camouflage, there was no place to hide and Dame Fate and Hag Death pursued her, their twin breaths hot on her neck.

. . . offworld foods she'd always wanted to taste simply because their names had been so exotic: cockatrice, day-diggers. And because she was lassari, there had been no money for such luxuries. . . .

The next shot found her. The grass was surprisingly

soft as she fell. It caressed her. The shunter, broken, bathed her with bands of sparkling brilliance.

. . . *and* . . . *and* . . .

The body of a woman was found the next morning by a caravan of spice traders moving autowains toward Sterka and the Port. The night animals had gotten to the carcass—a not particularly pleasant sight—but the traders, a stoic guild, threw the body across the back of a wain. After all, if she were of kin, her guild would wish to give final rites, and might pay for the body. The cinammon odor of the spice cloaked the smell of blood.

They found that the woman was well-known to denizens of the Port, and that she was lassari—a minor criminal record had made her face (what remained of it) familiar to the constabulary. They shrugged their collective shoulders, complimenting the traders on their generosity in bringing the body back and shaking their heads sorrowfully at the wasted effort.

Irritated that they had spent their time on a lassari, they left the body with the policing guild, who had the hospital nearby remove any useful parts and then dispose of what remained.

No one particularly mourned her death—and since murder is not always a crime in Neweden, no one bothered to look any further into the matter.

Hag Death was mollified.

The Thane lay on his bed. He pillowed his head with his hands, lying on his back, and stared at the reflections of a dim hoverlamp skittering across the bare rock of the ceiling. The top of his uniform lay discarded on the floor; glancing down, he could see the torso of a man still in fair shape, but the edges of the once sharply-defined musculature were being slowly eroded. A general blurring of tone, an indefinable sag—he sometimes wondered if it weren't more emotional than physical. The Thane would find himself, now and then, staring into a mirror at the reflection of his profile, seeking assurance that the stomach was still relatively flat and the posture erect, trying to find in that shadow Thane the echo of his younger reality, that earlier

Thane. Where was age, how did one see it? Was it a function of the hands, the face, the mind? Could it be captured and removed, could he rekindle the intensity?

It was distressing to him that only he of all Hoorka-kin could remember his father—his biological father—telling him tales of the long fall of Huard and how his father had been trained to kill Huard, part of a group of revolutionaries. Huard's suicide had destroyed that group's meaning and drive; his father's among them. He had wandered through the wreckage of a reeling empire, finally ending on Neweden to find himself a pariah, a social outcast without kin—and, as suddenly, as trade between worlds ended, with no way of leaving. The Thane could remember his father, who had been old when he was born, but it was a wavery face dimmed and filtered by distance. He had a holocube of the man somewhere, but it had been years since he'd looked at it, and kin do not honor their biological parents.

The chime of the doorward interrupted his thoughts. He considered rising to dress, then shrugged mentally, not caring to move.

"Come," he said. He sat up on an elbow and watched the doorshield waver and dilate. Mondom stepped through, her eyes wide as she tried to adjust to the dimness. The Thane could see her clearly against the corridor lamps. Hers was a full, almost stocky figure that—while feminine and graceful—still carried a raw power. Auburn hair was glossed by the backlighting, a frothy, soft nimbus. Her legs were trim and muscular, her hands at her side. The stubby fingers opened and closed. She moved into the room hesitantly, glancing at the hoverlamp on the ceiling, and then to the bed. She stepped fully into the room and the doorshield irised shut behind her.

"Damned dark in here. You think this is a cave?"

"Cute."

"An old joke, neh?" Mondom smiled.

"Yah. I can see you, anyway."

"So? What color are my palms? I'll bet you can't see that well." She held them out toward him. He saw a pair of dark islands, each with five peninsulas.

"Blue," he said. It seemed likely.

"Flesh. I washed the tint from them this evening—and

the dye was orange, in any event. Have you ceased to notice my appearance at dinner, or are your eyes failing you? Either way, I'm not flattered."

The Thane hmmed a reply deep in his throat. He glanced down the length of his body and saw the roll of flesh at his waist. He stretched himself and finally lay back down so that the stomach was again smooth. His own vanity amused him, but he made no move to ignore it. "Did you come in here simply to be flattered?"

"I need reasons to see you?" she asked, lightly.

"I suppose not."

With that, the talk faltered. There was a moment of mutual embarrassment as Mondom glanced nervously from the Thane to the hoverlamp. Then, hesitantly: "You haven't been much in evidence the last few days. Problems?" She waited, a beat. "As a friend, Thane." Her eyes pleaded with his.

"Problems," he conceded.

"The fight with Aldhelm?"

"Partially." He knew the curt replies were hurting her, but somehow couldn't bring himself to elaborate. He watched her standing in the center of the room, shifting her weight from one foot to the other, and he knew he could end her discomfiture with a word. He couldn't say it.

"Do you want to talk about it?" she asked finally.

"No."

"Talk sometimes helps."

"You really think it necessary? Talking won't make anything clearer, won't change situations."

"Maybe not, but it won't cloud things, either."

"Then talk." The Thane waved a hand and closed his eyes. Through the self-imposed darkness, he could hear her soft breathing, the rustling of cloth as she moved.

"You're letting everything that happens become some" —Mondom hesitated, searching for words—"some magical symbol of vague doom. I don't even know what's most disturbing, your twisting of small events into auguries of great import, or the events themselves. The Hoorka are facing a real crisis. We need a real solution. And you seem content to let Dame Fate twist the threads into whatever pattern She desires."

"As She always will do. Hoorka has faced crises before, and come through them." He spoke with his eyes clamped shut. He didn't want to see the concern in her face.

"And it has always been your guidance that led us."

Mondom came over to the bed and sat beside him. He felt the supporting field bounce slightly as it compensated for the increased weight. She touched his hand tentatively; then, when he didn't pull away, she let her hand rest there, covering his. All of the Thane's consciousness seemed concentrated there—he could feel the satiny texture of her palm and the roughness of the callouses gathered at the tip of each finger. Her hand was warm, with a trace of sweat, and his own hand seemed chill against hers: autumn and high summer. Still, he couldn't bring himself to look at her, though his eyes opened. He stared at the nether regions beyond the hoverlamp.

"Why these sudden hesitations?" she asked. "You can see what it's doing to the others." Her voice was gritty sand and fluffed cotton. "*You* made the fight with Aldhelm take on an importance beyond its true proportions. No Hoorka would expect you to defeat him in a fight at any other time—he's simply bigger, stronger, and more agile than you, and if that pricks your damned pride, I'm sorry. You insisted on turning it into a power play. If it *was* a symbol, you made it that way."

"It seemed necessary."

The Thane's voice rasped through his throat, rough and husky. But his eyes, finding her face, discovered it to be vulnerable and open with genuine empathy. His hand moved, a spasm, beneath hers.

"A reprimand . . ."

"Wouldn't have been enough," he finished for her. Then: "I don't know. Maybe you're right." Irritated, he moved his hand from under hers and gesticulated violently. The hoverlamp bobbed with the moving air as Mondom moved back in surprise.

"I don't know any more," he shouted. "I find myself wondering about the morality of what I've built here, wondering whether I care to have my name forever linked with that of Hoorka . . . Mondom, I'm tired. I find myself caring more about myself than for my kin."

"You've always masked yourself. I don't even know your family name."

"Does it matter on Neweden?" His eyes were pained. "They were lassari."

"I'd like to know."

"Hermond. Gyll Hermond." His voice dared her to comment.

Mondom shrugged. "It's a name. What does it matter that Hermond isn't among the lists of the guilded?"

"It mattered. You've never been lassari—your family had kin. You wouldn't understand."

"Perhaps not, but I can still feel your pain, kin-brother."

The Thane shook his head. "I sit here and make excuses for all my problems. I'm getting very tired—and I'm not senile, not in my dotage, not even particularly old. I don't think I've lost any mental agility I once had. And making you feel guilty about my background is just another ploy on my part. I surround myself with sophistry and easy motivations." A pause. He ran his hand through graying hair. "I'm sorry, Mondom. I truly am."

The Thane sat back against the rough stones of the wall, staring at the hoverlamp in the center of the room. Mondom reached out to stroke his cheek with her hand. The undepilated stubble dragged at her skin, and she let the hand wander from cheek to shoulder. She moved close to him, the bed jiggling as it took her full weight. Shadows merged on rock. She forced him to look at her, her hands moving in mute comfort.

He didn't encourage her. He didn't resist.

Mondom kissed his mouth, but his lips were unpliant; she could feel his muscles stiffen. Then, as suddenly, he relaxed, the tension sloughing from his body. His arms came around her, and he sigh-groaned as she clasped him. Her fingers searched for the fastener to her tunic, found it, and tugged.

Cloth fell away with a whisper.

His hands cupped her breasts, circled one nipple with a forefinger, and then felt the smoothness of her back. The Thane sighed. "I've missed you," he said in a harsh whisper. "I wouldn't let myself admit it, but I knew it inside."

"I would have come. Any time." Her voice was soft in his ear, and her hands roamed his body.

"I know. I don't know why—"

Mondom stopped his voice with her mouth.

Nine

Tri-Guild Church threw sharp-spiked shadows across the pavement of Market Square. The palpable darkness shivered as the crowds moved through it and lifted its borders onto their shoulders. Its keen edges and protrusions should have caught and impaled those walking below, but the best the shadows could do was impart a temporary chill, a premonition of unguessed doom.

McWilms entered the shade and immediately missed the sunstar—it was a chilly morning prescient with impending winter and snow. Though the sunstar lent a psychic warmth to the air, it seemed unable to warm the earth with its distant fires. Even the Hoorka uniform (with the red sleeve that signified his apprentice status: that would be gone soon, McWilms hoped) could only blunt the cutting edge of the cool wind. McWilms glanced at the spires of the church and shivered unreligiously. It was a massive building, ornate with flowering spires and graceless arches—he would be in its shadow for some minutes before entering the realm of the sunstar again. He cursed the builders for having chosen such an inconvenient site for their place of worship, then as abruptly asked She of the Five to protect him from his blasphemy.

McWilms did not mind hedging his skepticisms.

He moved through a welter of people, accepting the open area that seemed to move with him as part of the deference due him as a Hoorka. He had to admit that such things were aspects of being a Hoorka that thrilled him: the sense of grudging respect that other kin gave him, even as an apprentice. A young man with kin, such as himself, would under normal circumstances have far less status in Neweden society. But he was Hoorka, however lowly in that guild, and the fear of the Hoorka extended even to him. He had, now and again, deliberately sought out the more crowded streets of Sterka just to feel the aura of power that surrounded him; he would watch the people step—grudgingly—from his path. Fear laced with loathing would congeal their faces. It was . . . pleasant.

Today was the height of autumn's Market Days, when the outlying farming guilds brought in their harvested bounty. The streams of people that normally used the square each day was doubled and trebled, swelled into rivers, joined into seas. The noise grew as the Days went on and buyers attempted to wheedle prices from impassive and unsympathetic growers. Modified chaos: Neweden locals found the Days to be pleasant diversions in their lives, offworlders shook their heads and mumbled—inaudibly—comments concerning backward societies and their engaging oddities.

McWilms, after broaching church-shadow and entering the morning sun once more, found the truth to be somewhere between the two poles. He had been sent on an errand by the Hoorka in charge of the kitchens, and could not tarry overlong to enjoy the sights for fear of that master's justifiably-famous wrath. McWilms found a fishmonger's stall and watched the haggling. He pretended not to notice that he stood in an anomaly: a small open space all his own.

Behind a counter stocked with frozen sea creatures, the monger was arguing vehemently with a woman concerning the quality of a spiny puffindle that, admittedly, appeared undernourished. The monger quoted a price; the woman, in a greenish pearlwrap, snorted derision. She offered the man half that price, prodding the puffindle's side with a forefinger to make her point. Vapor from the cooling circuits in the counter swirled between them.

McWilms stepped closer, shouldering through the crowd with less courtesy than the guild etiquette required and watching as anger turned to carefully-masked irritation on their faces. People moved away with controlled distaste; the monger looked up from behind his stall. His features revolved through an interesting gamut of emotions: anger at being interrupted during a sale, quick shock at seeing the young man was a Hoorka, and finally a gelid shielding of all facial contortions that left his face blandly amiable. He stepped back and to one side, wiping his hands nervously on his stained pants; he ignored the woman, who glanced at the Hoorka apprentice, shut her mouth sullenly, then went back to prodding the cold scales of the puffindle as if trying to awaken the fish from liquid dreams.

"What can I do for you, young sirrah?" The monger's voice was deferential, but everything about him, from the skittish eyes to the tapping fingers to the manner in which he stood under his slickcloth awning, spoke of impatience, or possibly unwillingness to deal with Hoorka.

An older Hoorka might have been amused or angry in turn with the man's attitude, but McWilms was unused to the subtleties in other kin's reactions to Hoorka. He didn't notice. He smiled.

"I'd like to buy all of your stock for my kin."

Eyebrows sought new heights on the monger's forehead, then clambered down once more. He closed his eyes in thought. "For my entire selection? I'd have to charge you 150C. And that's a fine price, too."

"For whom, sirrah? You? I didn't ask you to empty the oceans. I can offer you 75C." The Hoorka master Felling had given him 120C, but had threatened to double McWilms's work load if he came back with less than 15C of that amount. The master was known for his gruff manner and gentle ways, but McWilms intended to take no chance on his good humor.

The monger looked pained at the offer. (And behind and around him, McWilms could hear the mildest undercurrent of speech as the kin around him realized that the Hoorka intended to buy all of this monger's stock. The woman next to the apprentice stopped examining the puffindle to watch.)

"75C wouldn't pay my transportation costs here, much less the rest of my expenses. Sterka is an expensive city in which to stay during Market Days, sirrah."

"Other people are selling here." McWilms indicated the gaily-colored stalls around the square. "I could see if perhaps their overhead is lower than yours."

The monger cogitated. "For the Hoorka—a fine guild —I could go, perhaps, to 125C."

Too slowly, McWilms started to turn away. The people crowded near him stepped back into those behind them, startled.

"100C, then," the monger called out.

McWilms stopped and turned around. "You'd deliver it to Underasgard?" he said over his shoulder, still poised to leave.

The pained look returned to the monger's face.

McWilms, hearing nothing, started to move away once more.

"I'll deliver, sirrah. For 105C."

McWilms stepped back to the counter. "That sounds acceptable," he said. The two finalized the arrangements and tabulated the fish the monger had brought. Scrip changed hands; as it did, people began moving away from the stall, going off to search for other mongers as it became obvious that the Hoorka deal had been completed. The pique on their faces was evident. Finally, McWilms put his purse back under his cloak and moved back into the crowds, walking in his inviolate space.

He went from the temporary stalls of the various mongers toward the street emptying into the square from the north, its taverns and small guildshops attracting a large share of the revelers. He had time, since he had completed his task earlier than Felling could have expected, and the sights were intriguing to a boy whose true family had lived in a rural district of Illi. Events moved at a quicker pace here in Sterka, and as a Hoorka-kin, he had the added thrill of fear/respect. The wares of the Market Days shouted for his attention. He could see, on a shop ledge protruding out into the walkways, a selection of offworld items imported by Alliance traders, a meatfruit ball with its scaly, yellowish rind, a pile of Bosich exoskeletons (spiked and brilliantly colored). The sculptor's guild had opened the doors to the studio adjoining the street; inside he saw apprentices polishing a huge lifianstone sculpture partially hidden in shadow—it seemed to be two men locked in a fervent embrace; one thin, the other stocky—and he heard the soft *tchunk* of a chisel striking the soft stone. From somewhere ahead, the breeze brought the yeasty aroma of bread, a free advertisement for a bakery. Sights, sounds, smells: Sterka abounded in them during Market Days. McWilms reveled in the sensory surfeit.

(Yet he hadn't noticed the person who watched his movements through the crowds. The man was dressed in the uniform of a guilded kin—a belt with a holographic buckle adorned his waist, but the hologram was shattered and the guild insignia that should have been visible was lost in a welter of varied images and depths—and the uniform was not of any familiar guild in Sterka. Not that this in itself was unusual during Market Days; travelers filled the city. The man received no second glances. A person, noting him, might think he came from the far south, for certainly no nearby guilds used such odd boot fasteners on their pants. That was as he wished it. As McWilms walked past him, the man abandoned his post by the silversmith shop and plunged into the crowd after the apprentice.)

McWilms was absorbed in the bustling of the Days. The sunstar spilled its warmth into the street as it hauled itself toward the tenuous pinnacle of the zenith. The apprentice had no mind for strife, and trusted the Hoorka-fear to keep others from hindering him. So he was unprepared to see a man suddenly stumble into the pocket of open space around him.

McWilms caught a brief, dizzy glimpse of blue-green eyes, clutching hands, and a broken holobuckle at the man's waist. Stubby fingers grasped at his clothing—heavily—and a booted foot caught his shins. McWilms stumbled backward, falling to the ground as the man caught his balance and plunged back into the crowded street. McWilms cursed and got to his feet (around him, he saw open smiles and —judiciously distant—a snickering from some onlooker). It was too late. The man was gone and the people standing around him were too closely packed to easily pursue the man. The apprentice dusted off his clothing, trying vainly to collect the shards of his wounded pride. He straightened his clothing where the man's fingers had clawed at him. Paper crackled under his belt.

McWilms pulled an envelope from where it had been stuffed between belt and uniform. He stared at it.

It was addressed, in a spidery hand, to the Thane.

"You've both seen the note. I'd like your thoughts on it."

The Thane looked at Aldhelm and Mondom, seated in floaters in the Thane's room. Aldhelm held the slip of paper in his hand. He looked down at it, his eyes scanning the words once more, and shook his head.

"So Gunnar would like to meet you privately," he said. "I don't care for the idea, Thane. No matter that he says he has information that might interest us. You can't go to see him or have him come to Underasgard. Vingi wouldn't hesitate to consider that as more circumstantial evidence against us, and he'd drag us before the Assembly on a charge of illegal conspiracy. He couldn't win, of course, but the residual damage that the charge might do to Hoorka . . ." He shook his head again and held the note out to the Thane, who reached forward to take it from him. "We can't afford this, Thane. And believe me, Gunnar will be trying to extract a price. He's no better or more altruistic a man than the Li-Gallant."

"You're not at all curious about this 'substantial offer for the good of Hoorka' or"—his fingers scratched along the paper—" 'information which may have the greatest import for you'?"

"I'm admittedly curious, Thane, but not enough to wish to compromise Hoorka," Aldhelm replied. "There are higher allegiances than curiosity."

The answer disturbed the Thane. He'd asked Aldhelm and Mondom to come to his rooms, thinking that perhaps by taking Aldhelm into his confidence he could bridge some of the growing rift between them—and because he knew that Mondom would understand that ploy and aid him. By the code, the Hoorka-thane was not bound to take advice from any other Hoorka unless he should call a full Council meeting. But advice was helpful—even if he had, for the most part, made his decision. If it would help the uneasy relationship between Aldhelm and himself, so much the better.

Except that it wouldn't work.

Aldhelm seemed only mildly concerned with Gunnar's sudden interest in the Hoorka, and was evidently disinclined to investigate this offer of his. But the Thane wished to know what prompted it. The challenge of the note tugged at him, as he knew Gunnar had intended it to do. It was full of enigmatic terseness.

No, he wouldn't let it endanger Hoorka, if that's what it came to; yes, Aldhelm was right about Vingi's probable reaction to any meeting between the two guild-heads. It would be a powerful alliance, that of the Hoorka and Gunnar's Ruling Guild. Vingi would be forced to deplete much of his resources and capital to defeat them should they join in actual treaty. Neweden might see a guild war to rival the Great Feud of the last century. If the Thane hadn't the vision of an offworld Hoorka-guild, hadn't the goal of making the assassins something more than a planetbound curiosity, it would be tempting.

Perhaps too tempting.

The possibilities were not attractive.

"I was thinking of possibly arranging the meeting, nonetheless," the Thane said. Aldhelm's face clouded over with the words; Mondom, sitting cross-legged in her floater, tilted her head in surprise. The Thane hurried to continue.

"I've no intention of actually dealing with the man. I simply wish to know more about this proposal. And I'm most interested in knowing what information he claims to possess that would make us consider such a rash move as to consider a proposal from his guild. The information—it might be important to Hoorka."

"But most likely not," said Mondom. She unlaced her legs and stretched them, folding her hands on her lap. The Thane could read those movements—she always tried to appear relaxed when her thoughts were actually in turmoil. It could fool those who knew her casually, but it worried the Thane. "I don't know if it's worth the risk, Thane. It's *Gunnar* that Vingi would prefer to eliminate, not Hoorka. If we can avoid angering the Li-Gallant any further, he'll leave us in peace. We've done nothing to anger him before now, despite his damned paranoia."

Aldhelm had turned to look at Mondom as she spoke. Now he glanced back at the Thane, nodding his agreement. "M'Dame is right, Thane. Let Gunnar wonder why we failed to answer his note. And salve your curiosity with your kin."

So we must disagree again. Perhaps I should give in . . . "I have to disagree with the two of you on one point. Vingi *does* consider us a threat to his guild, if only because —now that the possibility has occurred to him—we will always be a potential enemy for his rivals to ally with. It was through us that Gunnar escaped"—with those words, Aldhelm's eyes narrowed—"and just his suspicions are enough. He would like to see us unguilded and hunted down like lassari criminals."

"Does that mean that you intend to see Gunnar?" Aldhelm shifted his weight in the floater, a preamble to rising.

I should give in. Their stand makes as much sense as mine. The Thane nodded in mute acknowledgment. He waited for angry words, for violent disagreement.

Nothing.

Aldhelm rose slowly from his floater. A finger ran idly from forehead to the tip of his nose, then finally curled around his chin. He stood, stretching. "I still think it unnecessary and possibly dangerous to Hoorka. But I don't think I can change your mind, Thane. At least I haven't been too successful at that recently. I trust you have the good sense to avoid the meeting being made public—that's the primary danger."

"I intend to take precautions." *Is it going to be this easy?*

Aldhelm shrugged. "Then there's nothing more to say. I hope you dredge the information from the man. Good day, Thane, Mondom." He left the room, walking slowly. The door closed behind him with a sibilant hissing.

The Thane glanced at Mondom, catching her profile as she looked at the door. She must have felt his eyes upon her, for she spoke without looking at the Thane.

"He's right. You know it, don't you? The potential doesn't match the danger involved."

"I don't agree," he said, more stiffly and formally than he'd intended. It hurt her visibly, and he cursed his social clumsiness.

"Then, as Aldhelm said, there's nothing more I can say."

"Mondom, I'm sorry. I swear to She of the Five I am. I don't mean to trod all over your feelings."

"You never do. That's the problem."

She wouldn't smile.

The Thane had never met Gunnar before but had seen him—as had all Neweden—any number of times on Assembly holocasts. For all that, he had been prepared to see some vague difference in the man, some masked dichotomy between the image and the reality. Gunnar looked neither taller nor shorter, thinner nor more rotund than he did in the holotanks. He had the same affably neutral half-smile, the unsteady doe eyes, the bluffly handsome features and well-tended body of the holo-Gunnar. There was nothing about him to shock the senses and make the Thane realize that the man he was facing was alive and not simply another random arrangement of light and shade beamed in the holotank at Underasgard.

Their meeting seemed to be a clandestine cliche. They met in one of the narrow and dark alleys of the Dasta Borough of Sterka, a section of the city inhabited largely by lassari. The Thane had eschewed his Hoorka uniform, choosing instead a cloaked outfit of some silky material that felt strangely cool against his skin. Gunnar, waiting for them, was muffled in a dull wrap that twisted and knotted in an indecipherable pattern around his body. The Thane wondered how—if he ever removed the clothing—he would put it back on.

Sartas and d'Mannberg, several steps behind the Thane and in the clothing of lassari, stared into the semi-darkness around the Thane and Gunnar. Sartas held a wide-dispersion infrared beamer and both Hoorka wore night glasses. To them, the alley was a brilliant wash of scarlet and orange.

To the Thane, it was merely dim. A faint glimmer of city-light glazed the sky and sent down a weak glow. Sleipnir cast a harsh shadow ten meters or so up the sooty brick walls that lined the street. He could see, if not particularly well, the garbage wind-piled at the edges of the wall, the gritty earth of the unpaved ground, and the mortar falling in a brittle dust from between the bricks.

A chance meeting of strangers in a dismal landscape.

Gunnar spoke first. "I didn't really think you'd come, Thane." He smiled.

In the night, the Thane could sense that meaningless smile. Gunnar extended his left hand, palm up and the hand inclined slightly below horizontal—a greeting between kin of different guilds—a gesture of gratitude and mild deference. Should the thumb move any higher above horizontal, it would be demeaning for a man of Gunnar's stature; too low and the Hoorka would be insulted at the implication that Gunnar considered himself above him. Proper form dictated that the Thane should return the gesture, but he kept his hand at his side. Hoorka have no friends outside the guild: you may be contracted to kill them the next day.

"I almost stayed in Underasgard. My coming seems to be against everyone's better judgment," the Thane replied. His voice was dry and uncaring.

Gunnar withdrew his hand as it became apparent that the Thane would not return the gesture of peace. His smile flickered and returned. "So my own kin thought. *I* thought, though, that it might be to our mutual advantage. We seem to have a common enemy, Thane." Gunnar glanced about him, from the dirty walls to the two Hoorka standing behind the Thane. There, his eyes seemed to be snagged. He laughed, a short bark that skittered into moonlight and was shattered. "You don't need to fear me that greatly, Thane," he said. "There's no feud between our houses, our gods are at peace, and there are, I trust, no contracts on me."

"You can understand my caution. I wouldn't care to have the Li-Gallant become aware of this meeting, no matter how innocent it may be—nor do I think you'd find it to your liking either, neh? It would not only be the Hoorka that would come before the Assembly."

Again the laugh. "I have no doubts that he'd try to

break my guild if he thought it would serve his own purposes."

(And the Thane remarked to himself: I don't trust this man, don't care for his light-hearted friendliness or his handsome face. Everything about him rings false and hollow . . .)

"Your information, Gunnar?"

Gunnar shook his head, the smile—it seemed to be an unvarying feature of his face—moving with him. He stuck his hands between folds of his clothing, putting all his weight on one foot: the pose of a relaxed man. "You're impatient, good sirrah. The information will come to you. But you must listen to my proposal first. I'm sure it will be neither startling nor unexpected to you. Look at the present situation on Neweden, and you can certainly see that we are in a position to lend each other considerable aid."

Silence from the Thane. In the middle distance, someone could be heard singing discordantly, while overhead the roar of a transport from Sterka Port shook mortar dust from the parapets above them.

The Thane stared at Gunnar, waiting.

The man continued his speech hurriedly, as if trying to get all the words out before the Thane turned and strode away. "My ruling guild has a small policing force, unlike that of Vingi. If we were to gain a majority in the Assembly, if I were Li-Gallant, we'd need a larger, far more efficient force. The Hoorka could provide the nucleus for that. And if you joined us now, well, Vingi's people simply aren't the trained professionals of the Hoorka. Should there be, say, a bloodfeud between the guilds of Gunnar and Vingi—and should the Hoorka side with us—we might well be in a position afterward to amply reward our allies."

"Do you know that m'Dame d'Embry of the Alliance is considering letting the Hoorka continue our work off-world?"

Gunnar spread his hands wide, sweeping them toward the stars above them, pale through the miasma of Sleipnir's light. "Do you know the woman, sirrah? I think her influence with the Alliance is on the wane. Yah, she is well-known among the Diplos, but she's *here,* and Neweden is just another name to the Alliance rulers on Niffleheim. They've given her a token assignment where she can no longer bother them with her unorthodoxy. You think she'll actually be the key to letting the Hoorka go offworld?" Gunnar's smile became sad, his head shook. "I grant you, Thane, that the Alliance would be a huge arena in which the Hoorka could work, but Neweden is large enough, and you have the advantage of knowing *how* to work here. Would you pass up what would be almost certain success to chase a ghost?"

"Your spectre or hers, what difference?" The Thane shrugged. "And hers more closely resembles my own."

"Ahh, so the Hoorka can sting with words as well as weapons. Yah, of course I'm chasing my own dreams. And I'll guarantee you that my ruling would be better for all Neweden. *And* for Hoorka."

"Every ruling guild says no differently."

"The Neweden bureaucracies need us to function, Thane. If there is no government providing a stable economy in which the guilds can operate, then there is no payment for Hoorka. Or do your people enjoy killing for its own excitement?"

The last statement was couched in a jocular tone that belied its sarcasm. In another person, the Thane might have found it simply distasteful—with Gunnar, it was bald insult. The Thane eyed the man, wondering again how he'd managed to escape Aldhelm and Sartas. Dame Fate had most decidedly smiled on him, but She had a way of suddenly releasing those who relied too heavily on Her good favor, laughing as the unfortunate fell. The Thane would enjoy being there when that happened—he would enjoy it even more were he the instrument of the Dame's reprisal.

He wondered if Gunnar knew how close to Hag Death he was.

The Thane scuffed a foot against the gravel of the alley, deciding finally to ignore the insult and let Gunnar live. Aldhelm and Mondom had been right, and the worst realization was that he'd suspected that all along. "Neweden's a violent world," he said finally. "You've never drawn blood?"

Gunnar shrugged. "What guild-kin hasn't done so at one point or another? I can defend myself in a feud, if that's your meaning."

"You found it . . . pleasant? Unpleasant?"

"Neither."

"The Hoorka do their job on a contract. They don't do it for pleasure. But it would give me great pleasure to slay a man who slighted my kin."

The Thane watched the smile on Gunnar's face fade. The man backed away from the Hoorka a step before the Thane waved a hand in dismissal.

"The Hoorka have no interest in your offer, sirrah," he said. "You know the Hoorka code. I intend to continue to follow it."

Gunnar stood as if poised for flight. Without the smile, his face looked naked, the lips a trifle too thin for the full cheeks and strong chin. Slowly, the man relaxed as the Hoorka made no move to harm him. "I had to make the effort, Thane. For my kin. You can understand that."

The Thane nodded slowly. "I can. And your information, so that I may feel that the evening wasn't totally wasted . . . ?"

"Vingi sent another assassin to our headquarters. A lassari."

"You're sure it was Vingi? Lassari have been known to be foolish." The Thane thought of the man that had attacked him in Market Square.

"Do you know of a lassari that could afford a light-shunter, or that would have 100C in her pocket? Look around us, Thane. This is where lassari live. Is this a rich district where a person can afford to have the equipment to foil my detectors?"

"If you have proof of your charges, then why haven't you gone to the Assembly with the complaint? It's illegal to involve lassari in a guild matter. Declare bloodfeud. Or don't you care for the excitement of killing?"

Gunnar ignored the irony. He looked up at the light-smeared sky, then back to the Thane. "You underestimate the resources of my guild. And what this might indicate is that Vingi already believes the Hoorka to have allied themselves with my kin. Why else send a lassari when the

Hoorka are available? What's to prevent him from attacking the Hoorka in the same manner? The man's mad, sirrah. He no longer follows the dictates of Neweden society."

"I don't think his arrogance that blind. If he couldn't defeat *you*, then he'll have no chance against my kin."

Gunnar stared at the Thane. He shrugged, as if ridding himself of the thinly-veiled insult. "Granted. But it would still be a nuisance to you, would it not?"

The Thane wished himself back in Underasgard. The night had already depressed him more than he'd expected: the squalid surroundings, Gunnar's irritating self-confidence, a vague feeling of dismal failure—he wallowed in a gray ennui. The Thane stepped back, turning half away from Gunnar as the man suddenly stood erect and held a hand up to halt the Thane's retreat.

"Thane, I might be holding Hoorka's fate in my hands. The interested parties in this altercation have a meeting with the Regent d'Embry, if you recall. And I know that your men are flooding this alley with infrared light. What if I had the forethought to position a person on the roofs and film this little meeting?"

It was a measure of Gunnar's desperation that he used that ploy. If he had expected his words to frighten the Thane, to cow the assassin, he had seriously misjudged his mark. Already angered by Gunnar, the Thane put one hand beneath his flowing cape. His eyes grew cold, the lines of his face as deep as if etched in an ippicator bone. Sartas and d'Mannberg, sensing the tension, moved closer to their leader; the menace on their faces was open. Gunnar stepped backward once more, the mask of his face broken and fright written there.

"You'd find the Hoorka to be a strong enemy." The Thane fingered the hilt of his vibro. He spat on the ground. "You'd also delight Vingi by doing that. You'd spare him the expense of buying a contract for you. Or are you simply a fool?"

A direct insult was something that should provoke guild-kin into a feud. Words such as the Thane's were seldom tolerated. The Hoorka could see the muscles of Gunnar's body at war with each other, vacillating between anger and fright. The Thane found himself wishing the man would make a threatening move, so that he would have no qualms about ending the matter here. Sartas had a flat-camera with him and had been recording the meeting, for the Thane had anticipated Gunnar using a conveniently-edited tape of their meeting to blackmail Hoorka. It would be easy . . .

But Gunnar seemed to rein himself in. The smile made a weak return.

"Not a . . . *fool*, Thane." Gunnar stumbled over the word, emphasizing it. "Simply a man trying to further the influence of his kin. Something we would all do, neh? Neither of us can blame the other for doing so, can we? If I speak frankly to you, it's because of the importance of our actions. I mean no insult to Hoorka. And I"—he paused—"apologize for any insult." He bowed his head in submission.

The Thane remained silent, staring over his shoulder at Gunnar. Sleipnir peered over the lip of the buildings.

Gunnar cleared his throat, looking up again. "There's nothing for me to say, then. I think the Hoorka might have done well to consider my offer, but . . ." He shook his head. "Potok will be at the meeting as my representative. I refuse to face Vingi as an equal until this matter is settled. If you should change your mind, Thane, please inform Potok. He'll relay the news to me. Good night, and may Dame Fate smile on your kin."

And with an unhurried pace that the Thane admired despite himself, Gunnar strode past the Thane and the two assassins and into the maze of streets.

Ten

An armed escort met the Thane at the entrance to Diplo Center.

It seemed an indication of the times—to his knowledge, the Alliance had always depended on automatic systems to guard themselves against attack and unwanted visitors. He might have been flattered to a degree if he thought that he was the only one accorded such treatment, but the Thane wasn't quite so vain. It seemed more likely that both Potok and Vingi had been met similarly. The Thane, deliberately late as a minor protest, followed the Diplo guards across a grassed lawn and into the yawning maw of the Center. The huge edifice swallowed them without effort. The Thane ignored the curious stares of those they passed in the lengthy corridors or moving the opposite way on the slidewalks. When the guards shuffled off the walk at an unmarked door, he nodded to them with mocking politeness. His muscles tense despite the show of calm, the Thane activated the door lock and stepped through.

There were three other people in the room, gathered about a wooden table in an otherwise barren room: Li-Gallant Vingi, Regent d'Embry, and Potok. The Thane bowed to d'Embry—he hoped she knew of the contract the Hoorka had completed for the last Alliance Regent. The Alliance shuffled Diplos so often that it was conceivable she might not know of her predecessor, and it had been to a young and too casual man that the Thane had first broached his dream of an offworld Hoorka guild. An obvious truism, he knew; but much was at stake here.

The Thane seated himself, ignoring the presence of both the Li-Gallant and Potok, directing all his attention to the Regent as the most important of the people in the room.

She appeared impatient. Her lips were tight and drawn and her posture was rigid—she looked as if she might rise and stalk off at any moment. One hand fondled a carved medallion on a chain around her neck. From the sheen and ivory brilliance of the jewelry, the Thane knew it to be a polished ippicator bone, worth far more than its size might indicate. He couldn't decide if her irritation was truth or a sham, for he knew that the Diplos were trained in psychological subtleties and deception. That meant he couldn't trust instinct here; she might be leading him. That bothered him—the Hoorka preferred to be the manipulators.

The Thane examined his calloused hands, waiting for someone to speak.

It was Vingi who broke the uncomfortable silence, clearing his throat to gain their attention. "The Regent has asked that this be a private meeting rather than a full Assembly conference, a request I've bowed to, considering that this is neither an official trial nor a registered complaint. Thane, you recognize Representative Potok of Gunnar's ruling guild? The Regent wished the opposition party to have their representative here—"

"Hold, if you will, Li-Gallant."

The Regent spoke suddenly and coldly, her gaze drifting past the others at the table and then boring into Vingi. The pupils were gray, the Thane noticed, as frigid as the void. For the first time since he'd entered the room, he allowed himself to relax, if slightly. The Regent was obviously on no side but her own. She seemed to hold a weary contempt for the Li-Gallant's pomposity, and that could only be to Hoorka's advantage. "Everyone here is aware of the context for the meeting," she continued. "I'm interested in one thing only: the Assassins' Guild's credibility—and my ship lifts in an hour for a conference on Aris. Leave your local squabbles for your Assembly. Please waste no more of my—our—time with such things."

(Cold, always cold. Does it come from erecting an

Alliance from the scattered ashes of Huard's long-dead empire? the Thane wondered. They all seemed like her, at least to some degree, these people of the Diplomatic Resources Team.)

Vingi accepted d'Embry's rebuff with a curt nod. He again cleared his throat. "To the point, then, m'Dame. Isn't it true, Thane, that Gunnar escaped from two Hoorka while totally unarmed and helpless? Doesn't that seem a trifle odd or suspiciously well-timed to you, with all respect to the whims of Dame Fate?"

The Thane glanced at d'Embry.

She shrugged and rested her chin on a cupped hand, while the other toyed with the ippicator medallion.

The Thane leaned back in his chair. "Gunnar escaped, Li-Gallant. That's hardly in dispute. And so did Geraint Sooms, and Erbin ca Dellia, and several others over the last several standards. You seem to forget, sirrah, that it's part of the Hoorka code that the victim retains a chance of escape. We contract only to attempt a fair assassination, and our efforts cease when the contract day expires. Gunnar was intelligent or favored enough by Dame Fate to elude my people. It was *not* conspiracy. Anyone can escape the Hoorka, should it be decreed by the gods that he should. You might escape yourself."

"Someone paid, Hoorka-Thane. Someone paid for death, not sophistry and rhetoric."

"The person who signed that contract should be advised that death is not for any man to buy. Hag Death makes a jealous lover." The Thane glanced at Potok, wondering what emotions were hidden behind that man's intent and serious stare. It was an ill-kept secret, the identity of the contractor for Gunnar, but it would be improper for any of those here to admit that, by Neweden morals. Yet the Thane admired Potok's reserve. He steepled his hands as he waited for Vingi's reply.

Unconcerned. Always appear unconcerned.

"You're dangerous if you've allied yourselves with Gunnar," said Vingi. "I make no pretext of enjoying the presence of members of his guild in the Assembly, nor do I conceal the pleasure I find in hearing that others of Neweden feel as I do"—this with a glare at Potok, huddled deep in the recesses of his chair as if seeking some hidden warmth—"since they only impede Neweden's progress to prosperity. I don't know who paid for the Gunnar contract, obviously, but the outcome disturbs me. That is why I must make certain of Hoorka's role."

Unexpectedly, d'Embry broke in, her voice low and steady. "Li-Gallant, you should recognize one thing. The *Alliance* will work with anyone holding the power of Neweden. It doesn't matter to us whether that is you, Gunnar, or any of the other scheming little ruling guilds that proliferate here. We're concerned only with aspects of Neweden that touch upon the Alliance: your exports, your payment for imports, the maintenance of the Port, and your representation on the Niffleheim Council. What is important here, I stress for the last time, is the possibility that the Hoorka have placed themselves in a compromising position of support for one or another of your guilds. If they wish to do so, it's entirely their choice. It would mean that they would be restricted to Neweden, but that is all—as far as the Alliance is concerned. We would have no further restriction for them.

"Your men fulfilled a contract for the Port authorities, if I recall correctly?" D'Embry's gaze slowly moved from the Li-Gallant to the Thane. He realized belatedly that the last question had been directed to him.

"We were paid to remove a saboteur. Your predecessor paid with offworld weaponry. The contract was successful, as I recall. Mondom and d'Mannberg were the Hoorka-kin working that night. Yes, I remember."

The Thane watched the Regent's hand—tinted a faint blue as if numbed by cold—go from the medallion to the table. And then the Regent shifted positions in her chair, a slight movement, but so quick and sure that it startled the Thane. It was incongruous in comparison to her slow speech and deliberate gestures, not at all part of the carefully-nurtured image of an antagonistic older woman. It worried him—he wondered how else he'd underestimated her complexities. He'd made the mistake of thinking her two-dimensional, taking her aloofness as shallowness or —at best—indifference. He would have to revise that estimation.

And he realized that he'd missed part of her reply. ". . . considered allowing the Hoorka to accept offworld contracts, but this matter needs to be settled. There are other questions, of course. Can the Hoorka maintain cohesiveness on a larger scale? Perhaps you'll find you have to limit the contracts you accept, and in that case what would determine acceptance or non-acceptance? The whole question of your integrity would take on a new dimension. Can you maintain the para-military regimentation that seems to be the only thing between the Hoorka and chaos? What would happen when there is no guild structure in which to function? But these questions are to be answered when you are implanted offworld—*if* that happens—and obviously I can have no real glimmering of that final solution, and have no real interest in it. I won't be involved by then. So let us first settle this small problem. If the Hoorka can't function on one . . ." The Regent hesitated, and the Thane saw her swallow the next word. A derogatory adjective? And was that hesitation deliberate also? ". . . small world, then certainly they cannot deal with several." There was hauteur in that voice, the ingrained superiority of civilization to the rural, the backward.

Duel with her, then. Parry and riposte. But you're outclassed.

"Our kind aren't unknown historically, m'Dame, even on the homeworld. Are you familiar with the Thuggee of ancient India?"

"No. And our ancestors were once also barbarians. We've progressed beyond that stage, and no one should use them as an excuse." A pause. "Well, one would *hope* that we've passed beyond our old follies. But I'm not concerned with historical precedent. Your particular, ahh, commodity is useless if it becomes linked to a political cause."

Touch.

"If I may be allowed a moment," interjected Potok. He had been slumped deep in the yielding caress of his chair. He spoke from that same ultra-relaxed position, a body seemingly without skeletal support. "I'm closer to the problem in some ways than any of us here. It was, after all, the leader of my guild *and* my personal friend who was the target of this unknown contractor."

Looking at the Li-Gallant.

"It *is* one aspect of your code I would change, Thane," Potok continued, turning to the Thane. "Why not release the names of the unsuccessful contracts as well as those you complete?"

"The bolt that misses you in the dark can tell you nothing of its owner, sirrah. The code works, and I see no reason to change it. Nothing can be proved. I say Gunnar escaped us, as some contracted victims will do, and the Li-Gallant claims that we let him go free. We can argue the point all day, should we care to do so."

"That, at least, is true." Potok slid ever deeper into his chair. His chin rested on his chest. He seemed totally at ease with the room and the situation, and, because of that, certain of his position.

It suddenly seemed ludicrous to the Thane. *All of us,* he thought, *carrying on our pretexts of self-confidence, making sure that our posturings fit the image, that we stay in character. And how many of us are that sure of ourselves and not simply frightened actors? The Regent? Perhaps.*

Surely not myself.

Potok spoke again. "My only contribution to this meeting is to state that the Hoorka have not allied themselves with us. I'll state that under oath, if necessary. The truth is quite the contrary." His gaze flickered past the Thane. "Our records are open to Alliance scrutiny, m'Dame d'Embry—or to the Li-Gallant Vingi, if it will satisfy his curiosity. I've no love for the assassins—my kin-brother was almost killed—but they are fair. I'll grant them that much. Were I or Gunnar less scrupulous, I might be tempted to say that they *had* formed an agreement with us, simply because that would discredit them and possibly erase a future threat to my guild, especially when one considers that the contractor is evidently too cowardly to declare an open bloodfeud against Gunnar."

The Li-Gallant examined his sleeve.

"M'Dame, Neweden wouldn't allow the joining of our guilds," Potok continued. "We'd simply unite the other guilds against us and fall. Murder is too easy a solution here; it comes too quickly to our minds, perhaps because it is so simple. No, the Hoorka have nothing to do with us. My words should have some weight with you, Regent."

There were innuendos, shadows of meaning that colored Potok's words. The Thane felt helpless amid the possibilities. *Does he say those words hoping he won't be believed, since it's the obvious way for him to respond if he is allied with the Hoorka? Does he say it hoping that I'll feel indebted to him and Gunnar, and reconsider their offer? Or be less eager with a future contract? Is it simply that he can't miss the opportunity of contradicting and hindering the Li-Gallant?* He shook his head slightly. Too many possibilities, too many directions.

He had lost any semblance of confidence. It had drained away.

"It does seem to have been an odd time for your kin to fail a contract, Thane, considering the stature of the victim," reiterated Vingi.

You're right, Li-Gallant. The thought roared in the Thane's head. *You're right. Perhaps there should have been no escape, even if it meant violation of the code.* (And further inside: *No, how can you think that?* It was a small voice.) "I would consider that, instead, evidence in our favor," the Thane said, speaking from habit while the inner fight raged. "Even realizing the consequences, we followed the code."

"And around we go again?" The Regent let disgust show in her voice. She turned to the Li-Gallant, the medallion on her neck catching the light softly and throwing it back into the room. "You mentioned that you had a thought for deciding this question, Li-Gallant?"

"I did, m'Dame."

Both the Thane and Potok looked at Vingi, the Thane with feigned nonchalance, Potok with the beginning of some faint alarm that dragged him from the depths of his chair.

The Regent stood, quickly. Her tunic swirled, then settled around her in an unruffled perfection. Light shimmered from the fabric, and the pale yellow-white of the ippicator bone was set like a jewel in the play of light. "Good. Then I'll waste no more time with these semantic games. Since you've managed to fritter away my morning inconclusively, Li-Gallant, I hope your plan bears ripened fruit. I shall be interested in the results." She stared at the Thane for a long moment as her hand went again to the ippicator medallion. "If the Hoorka can't be indicted, perhaps you and I will talk further, sirrah."

M'Dame d'Embry, in a rustling of glowcloth, left the room.

Neweden rested uneasily in the twilight. The sunstar, declining with haste from the western sky, laced the horizon with brilliant scarves of farewell—banded azure, green-gold, and topaz bordered by brilliant orange—all drifting to gray as the star became bloated and oblate, a gelatinous mass easing its weight carefully onto the pricking spires of distant hills. The ghost of Gulltopp had its entrance in the east. Lights began to move in the streets as Neweden sought to banish the tiresome onslaught of night.

For Eorl, it was time to return to Underasgard and its eternal night.

Eorl had been visiting his true family—not that it ever seemed to be a pleasant task. In the two standards since he'd joined the Hoorka, they had yet to accept the fact that he had no interest in becoming an artisan like his true-mother (and she for her own part refused to see his lack of talent). As for his true-father, non-guilded himself and saved from the onus of being named lassari because of his true-mother's affiliations (it was this very law that made it preferable to marry within one's own guild)—his true-father would sit and watch their arguments without comment, his eyes dulled by too much binda juice. She persisted in viewing the Hoorka as a temporary affectation of her true-son that would, given time and much argument, wither and disappear like a discarded garment.

Such attachment to true-family came because both true-parents had been offworlders and did not entirely understand the rigors of guild-kinship. It was an onus Eorl had borne through his childhood, having to endure the taunts of Neweden children because Eorl lived with his true-parents instead of at the guild commune. He had not enjoyed that, and he did not enjoy the visits home.

And this day was no different from the others that

preceeded it. Eorl wondered why he persisted in taking the time. It was a masochistic relationship; he succeeded only in ripping open the crusted skin over the old wounds and in reminding himself of how those wounds had once hurt.

The visits always started off well, a glow of optimism born of distance. They'd avoid the sensitive topics with an uneasy adroitness until all the neutral, dull subjects were laid aside with a nearly audible sigh and someone (it was almost always his mother) would ask about the Hoorka or mention that someone had been assassinated by Hoorka-kin. The voice would suddenly turn archly cruel—had Eorl been involved in *that* killing?—and mention that it was a fine thing for a person who could have joined a respectable guild to kill another person without personal enmity or a formally declared bloodfeud. And the argument would begin, until mingled pain and anger would drive him from their house.

No, it wasn't worth the effort. Eorl suddenly realized that he had subconsciously arrived at a decision. This had been the last visit. He wouldn't see them again.

The thoughts held remarkably little sting.

Shadows raced eastward from the closely-packed buildings, clawing their way up walls or pooling in exhaustion in the streets. Eorl was in Brentwood, a dilapidated section of Sterka with some houses dating back to the Settling. It was reputed—despite the evidence in the scant and spotty Neweden archives—that the first ship had set down here, on what was once a hilly forest. The styles of that fabled period tended toward tall structures with decorative and non-functional facades. Occasionally, one would see a bas-relief with fanciful representations of ippicators or mythical creatures. Grotesques perched menacingly above the street and leered down at the passers-by—across the street from him, Eorl watched one grotesque scamper along the roofline, point, and jeer insults at him. Despite his melancholia, Eorl smiled—not too many of the houses still functioned that well. He gestured at the imp with a fist and the creature fondled itself obscenely and ran to the far side of the building. For the most part, the friezes of Brentwood had cracked and fallen as the machinery failed, and grotesques stared stiffly from their last posture or leered up from the ground on which they'd fallen. Still, seen in evening's half-shadow, the area had a gothic character that called racial memories from long sleep. Old superstitions seemed to walk freely here—and Brentwood had more than its share of bizarre cults and odd happenings.

But a Hoorka could walk anywhere. The aura of the guild surrounded and protected him. The deathgods smiled on the assassins. They were safe.

The streets were nearly empty—it was too late in the day for the neighborhood crowds and too early for the night denizens. Up the narrow, winding street, Eorl saw a woman pushing a floater across the intersection. Heads grinned and frowned from the floater, several dozen of them—it was a startling moment before Eorl recognized the pallor of their faces as being native stone and the heads themselves as gargoyle carvings. A few youths lounged in a tavern doorway near him, speaking in the tortuously slow syllables of people on a time-stretcher. They scowled—too slowly—as the Hoorka passed; not unexpectedly, since Stretchers made most people irritable. By the time they decided to confront him (Stretchers also having been known to make the user foolishly brave) he had passed them. He glanced back to see one of the youths open his mouth and raise a fist. The air around him seemed heavy—the fist moved ponderously. A wirehead, stumbling by the youths and lost in his own reality, attracted their attention then, and Eorl looked away. The head-carting woman had passed through the intersection. He caught a brief glimpse of her blue dress before houses blocked her from view.

It was not the most pleasant of neighborhoods. Yet he'd grown up here, while his true-mother's guildhouse had been located in the interface between Brentwood and a richer neighborhood. He'd roamed these streets as a child and then again as the leader of a band of unruly jussar. And then the guildhouse had been moved; while his true-mother followed her kin, he'd offered himself to the Hoorka. They'd taken him.

He knew the area. He enjoyed its defiance of Neweden conventions.

Yet even the most familiar landscapes can hold a surprise.

As Eorl came to the intersection, he heard the low chant of a procession of the Dead. He shook his head in disgust—the mantra was coming from the street he wished to take. Eorl had no wish to waste time waiting for the procession to pass him, and the Dead had an annoying habit of blocking streets completely, knocking down those who stood in their way and weren't nimble enough to dodge. The chant was louder—they were moving toward him, then. Eorl cursed and turned westward.

He strode into molten sun, his shadow long behind him. He shrugged at his nightcloak, tugging it into place over his shoulders. This street was narrower than the last —he thought he could reach out and touch the buildings on either side.

Eorl scowled, anxious to be home in Underasgard and irritated at the delay caused by the Dead. Their wordless chant pursued him.

There was no transition. One moment he was walking, and the next he saw vague shapes run toward him as his mind shrieked alarm. They came at him from all sides; a flurry of fists and limbs moved in a wash of dying sun. Hands grasped the Hoorka from behind. Eorl went with the attack immediately, planting his feet and pushing backward as he sought the vibro sheathed at his waist. Something (hot? That was his first impression) sliced along his back, followed by a sluggish wetness that was surprisingly without pain. He found his vibro and slashed at the attacker behind him, feeling the comfortable resistance of blade meeting flesh.

(Thinking: *how deep is that back wound? How much time do I have?*)

A man's baritone yelped in pain, retreating as Eorl pivoted to meet the others. But his body failed to complete the turn. Sudden white agony arced across his waist and stomach—another vibro—and his face contorted. Eorl doubled over in torture. He tried to keep his footing, to hold the vibro out as a symbolic resistance as they closed in on him.

(*How many? Gods, I don't know. At least let one of them precede my soul when I stand before She of the Five let my blood stain their gods it HURTS . . .*)

Something blunt and hard struck him from the side and

his kidneys screamed. He saw with terrible clarity a hand holding a whining vibro (scarlet in the last rays of the sunstar, shining), watched with open, amazed eyes as it plunged into his stomach. Thick and full blood welled over the hilt and down a long, deadly canyon as the hand wrenched the vibro to the side. Eorl felt himself falling, saw the street slant and then rise to meet him. There were more blows, more stabbings. In the end he no longer felt them, only heard the dulling sounds as the darkness deeper than the coming night closed in around him.

Then even the sounds were lost.

Eleven

"We have very little choice."

The eternal night of Underasgard: black cotton of darkness angry at being disturbed and held back by glow-torches guttering fitfully in their wall holders. And beyond where the torches glowed and people walked, the darkness spread its feather weight around rocks and slept.

In a room in the Hoorka section of the caverns sat the Hoorka: the Thane, Aldhelm, and a few others seated at a rough wooden table (made by a new apprentice whose true-father had been a carpenter. It was evident from the grinning joints between the boards that he had not inherited his true-father's craft). Cranmer, as always, sat unobtrusively to one side, watching the meters on his recording equipment as if his gaze would provide assurance that it would remain functioning. Mugs filled with newly-made mead sat like islands in gold-brown ringlets of condensation. A pitcher held more of the drink within easy reach—beads of the liquor ran from the spout to the base. The scent of honey freshened the air.

"We can assume that Vingi will sign a new contract for Gunnar." Aldhelm lifted his mug, sipped, wiped his lips, then set the mug down again. He wiped his hand on his thigh. "He'll give us our second chance to kill the man. This time, the Hoorka can't afford to fail."

"Even if success means abandoning the code?" asked Mondom. "You assume too much there, Aldhelm." She shook her head. Ringlets of dark hair shivered in sympathy.

Aldhelm slapped at the table. The meaty *thwapp* of flesh against wood cracked loudly in the room; heads turned as liquid sloshed over the edge of mugs. "I'm assuming only that we're interested in surviving on Neweden."

"Yah, but to abandon the code isn't the way of survival."

The Thane's voice, quiet but emphatic, gave him the attention of the Hoorka Council. As he spoke, one finger stroked the lip of the mug in front of him. "If we violate the code," he continued, "we've lost our integrity—which is exactly the claim Vingi already makes against us. Everything we've set up, everything we've struggled to build, would be a sham. And we wouldn't survive it."

The last sentence was directed to Aldhelm. The Thane's eyes brushed past the scarred cheek of the younger Hoorka, where a red-brown scab marked the line of a vibro gash. Across the table from the Thane, Mondom flashed him a quick smile. He returned it with a slight raising of his lips.

Aldhelm's arm slashed at the air. "The code *is* good for Hoorka. I don't dispute that. It works well enough for most contracts we deal with. But it has nearly failed us in the Gunnar/Vingi conflict. If it threatens to fail us again, we should be prepared to break those rules. Don't you see, my kin? We can break the code and live with whatever guilt that brings us, or we die. We'll accept whatever punishment She of the Five might send us. That's quite simple. The choice seems easy—now—to me. Thane, you remember your anger with Sartas and myself . . . I don't think you would have been too upset if we'd broken the code but killed Gunnar."

Yes, I remember. And he's right—I was more angry with the failure, and I had no right to be. "I remember, Aldhelm. But I also told you that I was glad you followed the code. I am not going to be swayed on that point—would Hag Death be pleased that you consider yourself her equal?"

"And if Gunnar would live, what then?" Aldhelm shook his head. "If the guilds ever thought we'd joined with another guild, we wouldn't have the people to answer all the declarations of bloodfeud."

A susurrus of argument filled the room as everyone tried to speak at once. The noise echoed through the cavern. In the end, it was Mondom's clear voice that broke through and held.

"I see your reasoning, Aldhelm. I do. But I can't agree that what you suggest is the right course. The code may be an artificial set of rules created by the Thane, but even he doesn't hold himself free to break them or release himself from them. For good or ill, we've based our existence around them, structured the fabric of Hoorka about the code. Sometimes the created must transcend the creator."

(At his recording equipment, Cranmer started, hearing his own words to the Thane so closely paraphrased. Had she overheard that, he wondered, or was that simply her own ironic choice of words?)

"Transcend the creator, or simply destroy him?" A beat. Aldhelm sipped from his mug again. "And his creation with him. *And* all his kin."

Mondom shook her head, exhaling loudly.

"Aldhelm, listen to me," the Thane said, fighting to rein in his increasing anger. *If I were stronger, this wouldn't be necessary. Once, standards ago, no meeting would have been needed or called. I wouldn't have explained myself to anyone, nor would they have asked—my kin would have followed without question. When did this vacillation start?* "Eorl was brutally murdered last night by a pack of cowards. No feud, no formal duel, no honor. Do you think it's because some unknown people don't like the code? No, I think it quite the opposite. It's symptomatic of our problem. We'll be beset on all sides if it ever becomes known that we've stepped aside from a rigidly neutral stance. Things such as Eorl's death might become commonplace. And the easiest way to insure that no other guild finds the Hoorka untrustworthy is simply never to sway from the code."

"Was it to retain our neutrality that you went to talk with Gunnar? Please, Thane, spare me your altruism." Aldhelm's voice held barely-controlled contempt. "Eorl's death may have been a chance accident. Look where it took place—Brentwood. I know we're all thinking of Gunnar and Vingi—but we'll pay the cost of Eorl's death when his murderers are found. My suggestion that the code be ignored wouldn't be common knowledge, not as long as kin can trust kin. Once, and then *only* if it becomes necessary, would we tamper with the code. No one would be shouting it through the streets of Sterka. It will save us more trouble. If Gunnar would live . . ."

"And if the Li-Gallant should want to kill another political rival, then what? Would we examine every contract with an eye for its possible effects on Hoorka and make *that* the determining factor as to whether a victim lives or dies? Damnit, man, we're only a level above every lassari cutthroat in Neweden now, whether you care to admit the truth of that or not. Would you sink your kin back down to that level once more?" The last words were a shout as the Thane's temper at last broke through his control, thrashing and boiling.

Again, Aldhelm gestured violently. What had begun as a simple meeting seemed to have become a confrontation, a power struggle, and the other Hoorka watched in silence: interested spectators.

"No, I wouldn't drag us down, as you say." Aldhelms' voice now matched that of the Thane in volume. "I can agree with Mondom on one point. The created *has* become more important than the creator. To insure its—*our*—safety, we have to *do* something rather than cower behind the sacred code. I'm sorry, Thane, but if Vingi feels that he has proof to link us to Gunnar, no matter how circumstantial or ambiguous that proof is, he'll not only have the Assembly outlaw us, but he'll have every assassin hunted down and executed. Your Regent d'Embry won't lift a hand to stop him—she won't interfere with local politics unless she stands to gain something by it."

"What does that matter, Aldhelm?" The Thane shook his head. "The Alliance has nothing to do with the contract."

"The Alliance can sit and wait to see if we're what we claim to be."

"And you counsel us to become something else."

"I want us to live. Look at the facts, Thane!" Aldhelm struck the table with fisted violence and rose to his feet.

(And what of the vaunted Hoorka composure, the icy

calm that is supposed to distinguish the Hoorka from other guild-kin? Remember that the thirty-first code-line states that one shows his inner faces only to Hoorka-kin. One can let occasion dictate manners, and one can be honest with kin.)

Aldhelm stalked across the room. His voice was suddenly low and tense with emotion. "Whatever the Li-Gallant's contract is, we fulfill it. That's my advice, and I know others here would agree." His index finger pointed at each of the Hoorka around the table in turn. "The Thane can't sleep with all of us."

The Thane's chair scraped against the floor as he stood in fury, his hand on the hilt of his vibro. He unsheathed the weapon. But Mondom was on her feet, also, before the low hum of the Thane's vibro began.

"Sit down, Thane," she said. Her voice brooked no argument, though the Thane remained standing, holding his activated vibro as he stared at Aldhelm. Mondom strode across the room to Aldhelm; she held her own blade, real-steel and nearly as sharp as a vibro, point foremost in her hand. Standing before the impassive Hoorka, her dagger touched cloth a few centimeters below his waist.

"You're not so good as to be untouchable, Hoorka." She spat out the words, her face twisted by emotion. "I can take you, and I think you realize that. If you'd care to chance your luck, just inform me and I'll arrange a meeting for our duel. Otherwise, watch your tongue—it seems to be disconnected from your mind. I *demand*"—her knife jabbed at him, pricking his skin lightly—"an apology for that last inference; or you'll give me satisfaction in a more physical way. Your choice, no-kin-of-mine."

Their eyes met and locked, and it was Aldhelm who looked away first.

Aldhelm stepped back from the woman, glancing down at her knife hand and the unwavering tip of her blade. He looked at the table, to where the Thane stood, one hand still on the hilt of his vibro, though the weapon was now in its sheath once more.

Aldhelm's voice was hesitant. "I spoke too quickly . . . I let my passion for Hoorka . . ." He shook his head.

"Mondom, Thane, you have my apology. My kin should feel sorrow for my outburst."

"I appreciate your fervor," said the Thane, "but if you say such a thing again in my hearing, you would do well to look to your blade."

"I spoke without thinking, Thane, as Mondom pointed out." He nodded to her. "But I still hold by the rest. Thane, you're floundering. You chastised Sartas and myself for failing to kill Gunnar, but you won't listen to me when I suggest that your chastisement was right, and that we should indeed slay the man. Do you simply enjoy contradicting me, or don't you know your own mind? We'll have another contract for Gunnar, if we know Vingi at all. If we—you—choose wrongly, then the Hoorka will die and become lassari scum. You've had my counsel. Make your decision as you will."

And with that, the Hoorka turned to bow to Mondom—her face still contorted with anger—and walked from the council room.

The closing of the door reverberated in the caverns.

That night.

Sleep never really came to the Thane. He hovered in a twilight landscape between sleep and waking, worry and oblivion; drifting back and forth on some tidal flow he couldn't control and prey to the misshappen creatures that lurked there. His thoughts were formless and chaotic, as elusive as the chimera of sleep that he chased: a gossamer wisp. The Hoorka lay on his bed, eyes closed to the gray roof of Underasgard, trying to keep his restlessness from waking Mondom, who slept beside him.

Visitors from the formless dark came:

He saw the vibro arcing toward Aldhelm's face, moving with an aching slowness and haloed with silver reflections as if seen through a flawed and cloudy glass. Though he tried, he couldn't hold it back or turn it aside. The blade cut into flesh, leaving a gash that grinned white and bloodless for a moment before—like lava from a fault—the blood welled and flowed. He dropped the blade as the blood stained the side of Aldhelm's face. He could only mutter, over and over, that he was sorry. Very sorry.

He was sorry that he remained so unsure, so uneasy in his role as Thane. The remainder of the Council meeting had gone badly, destroyed by the acrimony between Aldhelm and himself. The ghost of the younger Hoorka had remained in the room, casting a pall over the talking. Only Mondom seemed sure of her stand; she defended the code against the hesitant questions of the others while the Thane half-listened, lost in selfish brooding. The others . . . they didn't know how he felt. Could it be that it *is* necessary to sacrifice the principles that were their foundation? Could it be that survival depended on knowing when to set aside rules? No, please . . . no. If he felt he had a choice, he might choose to simply flee from it all.

The Thane, an ippicator, ran alongside a stream. Green foliage was crushed under his five hoofs, the earth turning black as they pitted the turf. He could sense it, deep within him: the Changing, the day the world would alter itself. The sky was heavy with feeling. Even as he raised his head to look, the clouds dropped the seedlings—the Breathers of Flame—and they descended to sit heavily on the hills above the river: the Change-bringers. He ran along the river, nostrils flaring as he breathed the scent of . . . something new, something fresh. He knew: this would change him, and his fellow ippicators knew it also; as he ran to the Change-bringers, others of his kind joined him. The thundering of their hooves shook the earth, sent birds into screaming flight, battered the trees. But the mud along the riverbank was treacherous. He fell, mewling his sorrow at not being able to see the Change. The muddy waters closed over his head as he bellowed in anger to the bright seedlings on the hill. Water filled his lungs, choking him . . .

The Thane looked into the waters of the river and saw that he wore the face of his true-father. The face was young —and *he* was young once more, just dismissed from the task force that had gleefully joined in the rebellion that followed the suicide-death of the dictator Huard. All his life he'd been trained and honed for that one task—to assassinate that hated despot—and now the madman had taken that life purpose away from him with one stroke of his knife. Chaos, his mentors had always said, is to be preferred to ordered tyranny, to routine tortures, to the rape and plundering of worlds for the satisfaction of one man's twisted whims. If chaos must follow Huard's death, then let there be chaos. But Huard had given no one that choice between order and chaos. He'd removed himself suddenly and without warning: the years, the indoctrination, the education, the training, the fanaticism—all were wasted, meaningless. Nowhere to go, nothing to do. He'd watched five of his teachers immolate themselves on a huge pyre, feeling that their earthly task was now finished. They, at least, had seemed pleased. Everyone with any power or ambition now greedily tried to snatch up their portion of Huard's riches. Garbage pickers. He'd drifted, a trained killer with no reason to kill, a weapon without a target. And he'd eventually come to Neweden, a nowhere world. Yet still a world that could tolerate him only because he was unguilded, lassari, and Neweden would take no special notice of him for that reason. Young, sure, proud—filled with channeled arrogance. Pride that Neweden slowly leached from him. He lived with a lassari woman already cowed from birth, and they had a son. To that son, he gave the knowledge, the training he'd had. On Neweden, if nowhere else, that would be a boon beyond imagination.

The young man had become much like Aldhelm. Aldhelm wasn't of the original Hoorka, who'd been little more than a motley set of half-criminal lassari. Most of those the Thane had originally gathered to him were gone now, dead or drifted away when they found that the code prevented them from grasping the power or riches they wanted. The Thane had been strong, he had been stubborn, he'd listened to no one but himself. Like Aldhelm.

(The Thane, restless, rubbed his eyes with knuckled hands. His movement stopped the dreams for a moment. He touched Mondom, felt her breasts and idly stroked a nipple until it swelled and hardened. He drew his legs up, cuddling with her spoon-fashion. He closed his eyes: the dreams had waited in the dark for him.)

Chaos *had* followed Huard's death, long decades in which worlds were sometimes out of reach, with no contact from the other worlds of humanity. Colonies were sometimes forgotten, sometimes lost. But the Alliance had come, loosely re-structuring the order of human space, allowing a proliferation of variety but placing the rein of order on chaos. Like all governments, it worked sometimes.

Sometime, he knew, he would have to retire and pass on the figurative sceptre. But there had always been one more thing to do, one more minor crisis to settle that, when ended, had engendered another. Now came a major cusp, and he was left with uncertainty and the onus of leadership. He had even lost his name somewhere along that path he'd followed and he was left with nothing but a name/title that was heavy with responsibility and—yes—vanity: Thane. He wanted the burden. He didn't want it.

He did.

Possibly.

In time, he slept, and the dreams left him.

And the next morning . . .

The annoying whine of the doorbuzzer woke the Thane. Mondom, head pillowed against his arm, stirred next to him. "Yah?" he said, tasting the raw settlings of last night's mead in his mouth. He kept his eyes closed.

"A new contract, Thane, with payment enclosed." The doorshield muffled the voice. It sounded dark and distant.

"From whom?" He opened his eyes to see Mondom staring at him with sleep-rimed eyes. She smiled, closed her eyes again, and snuggled next to him. From beyond the doorshield, he could hear the rustling of parchment, the tearing of a seal.

"It's from the Li-Gallant Vingi, sirrah."

"He's giving us another chance at Gunnar, then?"

Silence freighted with affirmation.

"The Hoorka-thane is here, m'Dame."

"Send him in."

"Yes, Regent."

The desk worker turned from the holo, glanced at the Thane, and pointed to a door across the lobby of the Center. In the high, vaulted ceiling, a glittering spheroid rotated slowly, sending winking lights across the walls and floor.

"Take that corridor, sirrah," he said. "Then enter the third door on your left." The Diplo, halfway through his directions, bent his head to sort through the microfiches on his desk. Varied lights from the receiver set into the desk swirled across his features. He didn't look up again, seemingly forgetting the Thane as the Hoorka, his face set in a scowl, turned and walked to the indicated corridor.

As he walked, he felt resentment building. The cool, impersonal efficiency of the Alliance irritated him like an annoying sound just below the threshold of hearing, sandpapering the bone just behind the ear. Walking into the Diplo Center was to walk out of Neweden's social structure and all that it implied. It took an effort to restrain himself from simply cursing and walking out again, except that he was afraid that such a grandiloquent gesture would be wasted on these people. They simply didn't care. *Hoorka do not beg*, he thought, but he was here not to beg, only to ask advice. He—and his world—simply weren't used to the cumbersome machinery that cocooned a sophisticated society: the words were Cranmer's, from one of the innumerable long talks that had filled their time together. They struck truth. Neweden had been too long isolated from the mainstream of human culture. Enough generations had passed for them to become used to their slower pace, for customs to diverge. Enough time for them to feel resentment tinged with envy at having to confront that sophistication once more.

The Thane counted doors: one, two (with the image of a mother reaching out loving hands toward him—Nordic model, indeterminate features, and not well-crafted), three—there a doorshield dilated, and he turned to stride through.

The Regent's office was not the mirror of his dream image. No, the room was too spartan, an arid oasis in the verdant desert of the Center. The ostentatious splendor was missing—the lack of it caused him disappointment rather than satisfaction, for it made it more difficult to maintain his scorn for Alliance practices. There was an animo-painting on one wall and a soundsculpture in a corner. The desk (from behind which the Regent motioned for him to enter) was stripped of any bureaucratic clutter. An inverted d'Embry stared from the varnished surface. She waved a yellow-tinted hand at the only other piece of furniture in the room, a hump-chair extruded from the floor.

"Please be seated, Thane."

He took the chair, feeling it move beneath him as it adjusted to his size. D'Embry folded her hands and rested her chin on them. "What can I do for Hoorka?" she asked, her voice as antiseptic as the room. The Thane realized now, having seen the environment in which she chose to live, that what he had taken for haughtiness was simply the manner of a busy and rather reclusive person. This office wasn't built for visitors, wasn't designed to accommodate anyone other than the woman who normally occupied it. The knowledge didn't relieve him. It was easier to dislike a cultural set than an individual.

"I assume you're aware of the new contract for Gunnar," he said without preamble.

A faint smile ghosted across the Regent's face. "My sources *have* mentioned it to me—and they've told me who signed that contract. Since there is no one else present but you and me, I don't feel any compuction to have it remain a pretended secret between us. I'm afraid I find the Li-Gallant rather unimaginative. I'd expected—and, I confess, hoped for—a more devious form of testing the Hoorka. I certainly could have devised a better method."

The Thane ignored the last sentence. If it were an attempt at humor, he didn't find it amusing; if it were the truth, he didn't care for her honesty. "Gunnar hasn't the finances to void this contract, no matter who has signed it."

"So you won't admit that the Li-Gallant is the signer? Ah, well. I do realize that what you say about Gunnar's finances is true. His guild is growing in popularity, but popularity, even on Neweden, doesn't guarantee wealth. He's not backed by the right guilds yet, especially since Ricia Cuscratti was killed and her guild withdrew their proxy vote from him. And that reminds me to ask a question. Does it bother the Hoorka that you are essentially working for the rich? It's a point of interest to myself and the Alliance."

The Thane forced his face to show nothing. He made his words sound as icily removed as the Regent's. "In most societies, wealth is a sign of power, real or acquired through other means. Those endowed with survival traits will survive, and money makes survival easier. That's one answer. And remember that we only attempt the assassination. Gunnar can—and did, in fact—escape us. And that's also survival, in a rude and perhaps crueler form. It's real, nonetheless. We've no desire to anger the gods concerned with the timing of a person's life. We are not images of Hag Death, and Dame Fate is our mentor."

"You don't find that philosophy rather simplistic?"

"I leave judgment on such things to scholars like Sondall-Cadhurst Cranmer. The code works, and Neweden accepts it as fitting into their structure. Surely you'll read Cranmer's treatise on the Hoorka, when he finishes it."

"I will." Flatly. Her chin rose from her clasped hands and sank again. Her tunic folded around her neck as she moved, and the Thane caught a glimpse of the ippicator medallion in the hollow of her throat. "It seems cruel," she said.

"The 45th code-line states that the Hoorka will not accept more than two contracts for the life of any one individual."

"Ahh, a change in the code?"

The Thane searched the voice for sarcasm and found none. "An addendum to the code, m'Dame." He spoke carefully, choosing his words. "The code is a growing entity. We've no intention of serving as a policing force for the rich *or* the poor. We endeavor only to be fair—and to survive." *There. Is that what the bitch wants to hear?*

The Regent shook her head. She used little of the current fashion—above the long and narrow neck, only the earlobes were dashed with color: yellow-white beneath the sandy-white hair. "And what of competition? If Neweden can live with one Assassin's Guild, why not two, four, ten?"

The Thane shook his head. "No one else could offer our training, our expertise—and still be content to let the victim live. Neweden won't accept an Assassin's Guild that guarantees death. That would break our concepts of honor, and anger the gods besides. The Hoorka bend that concept, but not dangerously. We fail in perhaps 15% of our contracts, but we *do* fail, and we refuse to overload the odds in our favor. So you see, m'Dame, I don't expect competition. If it comes, we'll deal with it then."

The Regent leaned back in her chair. "The Hoorka are interesting, if nothing else. I'll be honest with you, Thane. I don't think you'd survive for long offworld. Neweden is too precise and sheltered an environment, and that's what nurtures your organization. I think you'd be swamped with complexities once you step from this rural place."

"I would like the opportunity to make that experiment."

The Regent seemed to ignore his words. Her hand brushed the medallion underneath the fabric of her tunic, then lightly swept through the hair behind her neck. "There are a thousand problems I can foresee, one of the largest of which is whether the Alliance cares to have murder—and it *is* murder, however you dress and disguise it—walking the streets of other worlds. However, it's not really for me to decide. The ultimate choice will be given to the individual world governments, once the Diplos make the decision to allow the Hoorka to leave Neweden. And I must be honest with you and tell you that we've had inquiries as to when the Hoorka might be available. There is work for you offworld; for a time, at least."

Abruptly, she smiled, a spring thaw. For a brief moment, the Thane had a glimpse of the person behind the efficient mask she wore, and then it was gone. D'Embry was her removed self again. "You'd have to be carefully policed, Thane, always under scrutiny to be sure of your fairness. Taint the Hoorka name at *all*, and you become nothing more than hired killers—and you can find those on any world, with guaranteed results, also. Shorn of your nice little sophistries concerning survival and chance and the gods, you're nothing."

She sat forward, obviously waiting for some reaction from him. Her eyes wandered from the Thane to the soundsculpture to the animo, the points that defined the space of her office. He heard the sound of her feet whisking against the grass-carpet, a restless rhythm. The Thane knew, suddenly, that she would say nothing else of any importance, and the irritation he'd felt since walking into the Center grew stronger. Mondom had cautioned him that this meeting with the Regent would solve nothing, but he'd insisted on arranging it. He railed at himself inwardly. He'd thought he could tell the Regent of the internal conflict that Hoorka faced, make her aware of the way Aldhelm felt and perhaps gain Alliance support for being open and honest, but no . . . She was already unsure of Hoorka and the idea of their working offworld, and any admission of doubt in Hoorka's ranks would mean that they would be confined to Neweden forever. No, he couldn't tell her. Yes, he'd nearly made another error in judgment. *How can I call myself Thane? I should return to the old name and stop this nonsense. The weariness would go away.* And yet he knew he couldn't do that. His pride would wrestle the guilt and strangle it. It was *his* organization—he'd built it and it was only fitting that, if it were to be destroyed, he would be the agent of that destruction.

None of the arguments convinced him.

He felt only doubt.

"If Gunnar dies, what will that prove to you, m'Dame?" His control was faltering. He could feel his voice beginning to rise in pitch and vehemence, and he could do nothing to stop it. Restless, he stood and walked over to the animo-painting, touching the surface with one tentative finger. It felt oily and slick, but his fingertip was dry when he pulled it away. Illusion. He turned to face the Regent.

"If Gunnar died, would that prove Hoorka's innocence?" he asked. "If he lives, would that signify guilt? Is that to be the measure of our judgment?"

M'Dame d'Embry barked a short and unamused laugh. Her feet slapped at the floor. "If he dies," she replied, "it would seem to me that you have no ties with Gunnar—or that your instinct for survival is higher than any artificial loyalty to his guild. Have you ever met the man, incidentally?"

For a brief second, the Thane wondered if she knew of his encounter with Gunnar. But she went on. "It would be quite a coincidence if he lives, given the odds. Doesn't that make sense to you?"

"I've had others say much the same." Thinking of Aldhelm.

"That I can understand." The Regent pressed a contact underneath her desk. The wall to her left depolarized and a lemon wash of sunlight flooded the room. The Port basked in afternoon sun. Both the Thane and the Regent looked at the scene: Neweden metropolitan pastoral. The Thane looked away first.

"It's still possible Gunnar may escape, m'Dame. Dame Fate smiled on him once before, and may again. His odds remain the same as the last contract, and he escaped us then."

"Which is what began this entire uproar. Are you warning me to expect him to slip past you once more?"

"The victim always has his chance."

"Even Gunnar? When the Li-Gallant will be very angry?"

"Yah."

"That is good, I suppose." Unconcerned, she watched the bustling disorder of the Port outside. Then, as if she was suddenly reminded of something: "Would you care for tea or breakfast? I've yet to eat today." Again, she smiled at him, but this smile had the plasticity of a professional tool, a rehearsed gesture.

"M'Dame, all I wish to know is whether you'll give consideration to our request to be allowed offworld—*if* the Hoorka can prove our innocence to your satisfaction."

"And if the answer would be, ahh, no?" She turned to him, the smile still on her face. The Thane suddenly remembered where he'd seen its twin, on the face of Gunnar.

He chose his words with care, speaking slowly. "Then the Hoorka would be compelled to do whatever best suits them for their continued existence on Neweden. I won't allow the Hoorka to die, m'Dame."

D'Embry nodded, but her mind seemed elsewhere. "Thane, I promise you only that we will be watching this very carefully."

"But you'll watch?"

The Regent nodded her head. She looked once more at the scene revealed in her window.

"Nothing is certain in this world, Thane. Huard thought his empire would last centuries—it died with him. I once thought that I would be satisfied with the span of years given to me." She turned back to him, and the smile had gone sad and genuine. "You may rest your mind on that one point, Thane. We will watch."

Twelve

It was perhaps a measure of Gunnar's altruism that, when the contract was made known to him, he immediately sought refuge in solitude rather than remaining with his guild-kin.

Or—perhaps more likely—those kin, fearing for their own lives, simply refused to aid him and forced him to flee. The truth was never revealed afterward.

Whatever the reasons, it made the task simpler for the Hoorka. They had been forced to storm citadels of resistance before and it had always been costly in terms of lives, even those of Hoorka-kin. It didn't often happen—the Hoorka, by the code, would make no attempt to deliberately kill anyone but the contracted party. Neither would they do anything to endanger their own lives; if that meant others must die, then it would be so. It was, then, with a certain amount of relief on everyone's part that the news was received: Gunnar had fled—alone—to the forested ridges of the Dagorta Mountains. Stone could hide Gunnar, but stone wouldn't suffer from misdirected stings or a vibro gone amiss.

The report from the shadowing apprentices stated that Gunnar had carried with him neither weapons nor body-shield. The Khaelian daggers were once again laid out for the use of the Thane and Aldhelm—for the Thane had once more changed the rotation of the Hoorka. It was true that the two Hoorka who owned that turn—Ric d'Mannberg and a young woman named Iduna—protested the change, but the Thane was adamant. He told the Hoorka council that the assassins would send their two best representatives. Privately, the speculation was that the order had been shuffled so that the Thane could have the advantage of Aldhelm's skill while keeping him under observation. After all, they said, wouldn't the two most accomplished and skillful kin have been Aldhelm and Mondom?

It was not far past midnight when the Thane and Aldhelm caught up to the apprentices. One of the shadowers gave them a final report and traced on a map the trail Gunnar had taken and where he'd last been seen: he was a few kilometers away and, they said, showing signs of tiring. Another apprentice would be awaiting them not far ahead.

The Thane shrugged his nightcloak over his shoulders and stared into the rustling darkness that flowed under the trees. A cry from some nocturnal animal shrilled nearby, and starlight brushed a white-blue patina on the edges of the foliage. Sleipnir was just rising above the slopes but its light barely reached the clearing in which they stood, though the trees upslope cast futile long shadows into the valleys.

"Let's go, then," said the Thane. He turned to the apprentices and handed the map back to them with a nod. "We'll contact you if we need assistance with the body. Keep the flyer in the vicinity, in any case. It's been fueled, and the kitchens have provided a hot meal for you."

"Yah, Thane. Good luck to you both." The apprentices, in a shivering of darkness, left the clearing. The moon eased itself higher and the tops of the trees were touched with its brilliance.

Without a backward glance at Aldhelm, the Thane set off into the forest, closely followed by the other assassin. Both knew that nothing had been decided. Their ride to the foothills of the Dagortas had been silent, each of them content to think his own thoughts rather than dealing with pleasantries and inconsequential topics, all the while skirting the areas that caused pain. The Thane knew he should have spoken and tried to lance that wound before they were in the field, but he found himself unable to begin. He'd spent the flight staring at the moonlit landscape below. For punishment, Dame Fate now sent to him the spectres of his own fear and guilt. They chased him, even as he pursued Gunnar.

The trail had been marked by the apprentices—luminous patches that adhered to the trees or glowed in the dirt. The path meandered up and down the rough slopes, always leading deeper into the forest. It seemed obvious that Gunnar had planned this flight well. The cover was thick and abundant, and their quarry would be difficult to track down, since the code forbade their use of infrared devices when the victim was unarmed and unshielded. Ahead, if their map was accurate, the ground cover would thin out as the mountains began to rise in earnest to the heights—but there they would be forced into a slower pace because of the slopes.

The Hoorka said nothing. They used their energy only for pursuit and left their thoughts unvoiced. The Thane's apprehensions gave that silence no peace. He wondered what Aldhelm would do, and his mind provided him with frightening scenarios. He wondered whether he could really stop his kin-brother or whether he even wished to do so. For the first time in his memory, he could feel a situation controlling him, rather than the reverse. He hated that sense of frustration and blamed himself for its presence. He glanced back at Aldhelm, but the Hoorka seemed intent only on following the track of the apprentices—*his* harbored doubts, if any, seemed well-hidden. The Thane envied Aldhelm his seeming peace.

Three hours later, they came upon fresh traces of Gunnar's flight—a rudely trampled section of underbrush. The scent of broken milkpods was heavy in the area, and the whitish secretion from the plants slid stickily down the sides of the broken stalks. The remaining apprentice, McWilms, was waiting there for them. He leaned against a gnarled treetrunk, his breath labored and sweat from his open sleeves steaming in the night air—it was far too chilly for the summer attire: the Thane shivered in sympathy.

McWilms greeted them, then pointed to his left. "Gunnar's not far ahead. I was within sight of him not ten minutes ago. If you continue at your present pace, you'll catch up to him shortly. He seems tired, but he's not slowing as much as I'd expected. He's in good shape, sirrahs."

"Hag Death can chase a man beyond his normal limits. Is there anything else we should be aware of?" The Thane and Aldhelm both crouched down, stretching tired legs and regaining their breaths.

McWilms started to shake his head, then shrugged and gave a sheepish grin. "Not really, Thane. I once thought I heard a movement behind me, and turned to see what I thought was a small globe in the air . . ." He laughed in short, quick gasps. "But it was gone before I could even be certain I truly saw it. It was probably nothing: the moonlight, a reflection, fatigue and Sirrah Felling's bad cooking . . ."

The Thane glanced at Aldhelm with apprehension, but the assassin didn't seem to be listening to the conversation. Aldhelm was staring upslope to the path Gunnar had taken. The Thane felt his stomach knot with sudden tension as possible implications occurred to him. *Hover-holos. The Alliance could be watching. She said they would.* Possibilities. He wished he could believe in McWilms' reflections.

Still, he said nothing of this to the others. They dismissed McWilms, the Hoorka rising to their feet as the apprentice took his leave.

They followed the spoor of a desperate man, now; a man who knew he was being followed and who left behind the detritus of panic: broken twigs, a fragment of neo-cloth impaled on thorns, a muddy slope furrowed by fingers grasping for holds. The forest thinned, the trees moving further apart as if tired of each other's company. Moonlight dappled the ground as they crossed rock- and boulder-strewn fields carpeted with thick grasses that clutched at their nightcloaks as they passed. Twice, they caught a glimpse of a figure before them; each time it disappeared again, rounding a boulder-fall or passing a shoulder of a hill. Gunnar was moving with a certain confidence, keeping the Hoorka a constant distance behind him. They saw no indications that he was tiring now. The situation frustrated the Hoorka and profited Gunnar, for dawn was not far distant. Aldhelm cursed openly and exhorted the Thane to move faster. Their breaths were ragged and loud, misting in the early morning coolness.

"Aldhelm, can you see him?"

"No, Thane."

"Damn him." The Thane fingered the hilt of his vibro, stroking the well-used leather of the scabbard. He'd begun to wonder if there would come an opportunity to use the weapon tonight—and, if that were true, whether there would ever be another chance for Hoorka.

"He can't be too far ahead, Thane, and he'll have to rest soon. He can't keep up this pace." The last sentence had the intonations of a prayer.

"Nor can we."

Aldhelm looked back over his shoulder, standing a few meters up from the Thane. Sleipnir arced flame in his eyes. "Do we have a choice, Thane? You know what this contract means to Hoorka. If you can't keep pace with me, I'll go on alone."

"Aldhelm"—the Thane spoke wearily as he felt the old argument starting again—"remember the code. Please, kin-brother. We don't *have* to be this concerned about the victim. If he lives, he lives—it is Dame Fate's decree. It shouldn't matter to us." *No, but it does. You know that as well as Aldhelm. Why do you lie to Aldhelm when he knows that you don't believe your words any more than he does?*

"If Gunnar lives, we die. That's a decree I won't accept." Each of the last words was uttered in an explosion of breath, the syllables separated by silence. The grass beneath them rustled with harsh whispers. "We've gone over this point too many times, Thane. You can't deny that you think I'm right. Gunnar *has* to die tonight, no matter how that's accomplished. He's even helped us. Look around. There will be no witnesses here."

The Thane shook his head, refusing to acknowledge the truth of Aldhelm's words. Yet the Hoorka's reasoning had taken root in the uncertainty of his mind. "No," he began, half-heartedly.

"Yes!" Aldhelm cut in sharply. "You've become . . . I don't know. Soft, perhaps. You're certainly not looking at this realistically. And I'm not the only Hoorka-kin who feels this way." Aldhelm spoke in almost a pleading tone, and with a touch of sympathy that hurt the Thane more than his former harshness.

Of course he speaks harshly—I was never gentle with him, but always masked affection with gruffness. I taught him, and can one blame the pupil for emulating the teacher?

The Thane stared at the rocks about them, not wanting to speak. No, he couldn't see any sign of the watching eyes that m'Dame d' Embry had hinted would be there; no, there was no sign of Gunnar. "And if the Alliance is watching?" he asked finally.

"It's a risk we have to take. She of the Five will watch for us." Aldhelm's voice softened, but his eyes were hard and unrelenting. "I've nothing but respect for what you've done in the past, Thane. Leave, if you don't want to be sullied by this, but Gunnar will die tonight."

So easy. It would be so easy to listen to those words and walk away. All I need do is acknowledge that I've lost and Aldhelm deserves to be Thane. And perhaps he does . . .

"We lose our integrity either way, Aldhelm." The Thane's voice was touched with a weariness beyond the physical. He continued the dispute more from duty than conviction.

"Would you have integrity or survival? You heard it said the other night—the created must transcend the creator. And his rules."

"Or is it simply that you don't trust those guidelines, Aldhelm? If so, *you* are the betrayer of your kin." The Thane scuffed his boots against the ground. Gravel rasped against leather. He was anxious to move on. The longer they delayed, the more chance Aldhelm would need to put his ideas into reality.

Aldhelm, perhaps sensing the Thane's thoughts, turned and walked away without answering the Thane's last comment. The Thane watched him go. He put his hands in the pockets of his nightcloak, shifting his weight from one leg to another. He looked at the ground, then at the dwindling back of his kin-brother.

Then, slowly, he followed.

It was nearing dawn when they finally saw Gunnar once more. The man was scrambling up a ridge many meters above them, a deeper darkness etched against a satin sky. Either he couldn't see the assassins below him—wrapped as they were in their nightcloaks—or he no longer cared. He glanced downward several times, but made no move to seek cover. He fought his way upward. The stillness carried the sound of falling pebbles to the Hoorka.

"We have to get closer, Aldhelm. The daggers won't reach him at this distance."

Aldhelm made no reply. He stared at the figure above him as if the intensity of his gaze could halt the man's flight. Then he swept his nightcloak over one shoulder and drew an instrument from his pack. It glistened metallically in the moonlight. The Thane recognized it with a chill—an aast, a weapon that did for sonics much what the laser does for light—and he knew the charade was over.

"Aldhelm, Gunnar has no shield. An aast . . ." And he knew that Aldhelm was aware of that, and that he was simply wasting his breath.

Aldhelm fitted the power pack into its sockets and aligned the sights. A high keening wail like distant death came from the shielding of the weapon—Hag Death's cry.

"The code, man—"

Aldhelm whirled, his nightcloak moving. "*Damn* your code!" His lips were drawn back from his teeth in a grimace. He turned and sighted down the barrel. Above them, Gunnar reached for a handhold.

"The Alliance, then!" The Thane's voice was loud with desperation, though his mind told him to let it go, to be silent and watch as his days as Thane ended. "Think, kin-brother. They might be watching. D'Embry told me, promised me . . ."

Aldhelm shouted. "*No!*" A screech, a scream; the word struck rock and echoed through the peaks nearby. Against the stars, Gunnar turned, startled.

"Aldhelm, the Regent will protect us if we follow the code. I feel that to be true."

"I can't believe that, Thane. I'm sorry." Aldhelm held the aast in position, waiting.

And, at once . . .

Gunnar stood, momentarily a silhouette against the night sky. Aldhelm's finger convulsed on the triggering mechanism and a banshee howling cleaved the heavens. The Thane tugged at his side and loosed a dagger.

Aldhelm fell, his cry of rage shocking the mountainside.

Gunnar scrabbled his way to the top of the ridge and over.

It was done.

Her gray eyes watched with bland interest, a cool amusement. Head and shoulders; her features floated in the holotank like a dismembered corpse, the ivory sheen of the ippicator medallion bright against her sallow skin.

"So, Thane, it is over?"

He shrugged. "Yah. And you saw the hunt, m'Dame?"

D'Embry nodded. "I just ran the film through a viewer here—I assume that the one apprentice spoke to you of the hover-holos, since it did appear that he saw them. At that point, they were near Gunnar."

"He mentioned them." The Thane sat before the holotank, waiting. The call from the Regent d'Embry had been waiting when he'd returned to Underasgard. He supposed that he should be feeling apprehension and anxiety as he waited for her to speak, but he was too tired. He sat slump-shouldered in his chair. He felt surprisingly little at the moment. "And what of the film, m'Dame? How does it reflect on Hoorka?"

"Accurately. And interestingly." Her hand appeared at the bottom of the holotank, fingering the ippicator bone that hung there. Suddenly noticing her own gesture, she held the bone out to the Thane. "You Hoorka remind me of the ippicator, you know. An odd combination of features that doesn't seem viable, yet you exist."

"The ippicator died."

"So must we all, sirrah." She let the medallion drop against her throat once more. "That was close, Thane. Very close."

"You've made a decision, then?" He didn't care what

the answer was. He swore by She of the Five that he didn't care.

"I have some contracts here for you to examine once you come to the Diplo Center again." She did not smile. "I'm not sure I approve at all personally, but I can't in conscience delay any longer. That news should cause rejoicing among the kin, neh?"

He should have felt vindication. He should have run shouting for Mondom and his kin. Instead, he sat and stared at the mud on his boots.

Aldhelm awoke with the unsmiling face of the Thane hovering above him. Beyond the face he could see the fissured walls of Underasgard. He felt the coarse nap of a blanket against his arm, and to his ears came the faint sound of voices beyond the closed door of the room. Alive, then, he thought. Alive. He closed his eyes, inhaled, and opened them again.

The Thane was still there.

His face evidently echoed his surprise and relief at finding himself in other than the Hag's domains, for the Thane moved away and spoke.

"That's right, Aldhelm. You're back in the caverns. And you're still breathing. You may thank Dame Fate that I'm still capable of disabling a man without killing him."

With an effort, Aldhelm managed to struggle to a sitting position—the Thane, seated on a floater next to the bed, made no move to help him. Something tugged at Aldhelm's side and he grimaced at the sudden shock of pain. Burrs from the Dagorta underbrush dotted his clothing and the nightcloak laying across the foot of the bed. A med-kit weighted down his chest, the pinpricks of the IVs giving him a vague discomfort. His mouth was dry and stiff. His words rasped and scraped their way from his throat.

"The contract . . . ?"

The Thane shrugged. "Gunnar lives. Still."

"And the Li-Gallant Vingi?"

"As you might expect, he is rather perturbed. But he can do nothing. The Assembly will protect us. The other guilds were given a full report by the Diplos."

The Thane found himself reluctant to talk. Here was

his revenge, and yet he was reticent to flaunt it in Aldhelm's face. He forced himself to continue. "The Alliance had been watching, as I said they might be. The Regent showed Vingi their record of the night, and distributed copies to other guilds, here in Sterka at least. Vingi is satisfied —publicly."

The Thane's gaze was like the sting of a weapon.

"I did what I thought best for Hoorka and my kin," Aldhelm said. "By She of the Five, I thought I was right."

"Really?" The Thane couldn't keep the sarcasm from his voice.

Before Aldhelm could reply, a young apprentice knocked at the door and entered the room, the light of the main caverns flooding in behind her. She bent her head in salutation. "Thane Mondom has received a new contract, sirrah. She'd like you to see it."

"Tell the Thane I'll be there in a moment."

The apprentice bowed once more and left them. Silence threatened to smother them.

It was several moments before it was broken. "Thane Mondom?" Aldhelm's voice was a fragile melding of melancholy and question.

"I—" A pause. "I dealt poorly with this whole situation. If I'd been a stronger leader, perhaps you wouldn't have had a dagger in you, perhaps Eorl wouldn't have been killed. And Mondom is capable, perhaps not as good a knife-wielder as you, but she follows the code." The Thane shrugged. "So I'm no longer the Thane. I've taken up my true name once more: Gyll—though I've heard some refer to me as Ulthane. An emeritus title for the creator, neh?" He smiled, wanly.

Again, silence came between them. There was nothing to say. After a moment, the Thane nodded his leave to Aldhelm and left the chamber.

Cranmer was waiting for him outside. The scholar had evidently been repairing his voicetyper—ink stained his forehead. The Thane smiled at the sight, and Cranmer inclined his head toward Aldhelm's room.

"How is he?"

"Upset."

"I don't blame him, but he'll understand in time, Gyll.

You did what you needed to do. Events bore you out." Cranmer's hand grasped the Hoorka's arm in affection and concern. "You saved Hoorka from extinction. Aldhelm would have destroyed your kin."

"I didn't do what I did to save Hoorka. I did it to stop Aldhelm. There's a difference. And I don't care for it."

Cranmer shrugged. "Possibly . . ." He shook his head. "In any event, Mondom—I mean, *Thane* Mondom—asked me to be sure that the apprentice delivered her message and didn't get waylaid in the kitchens."

"It was delivered. I'm going there now. You can do something for me, also."

"What, my friend? Clean the kitchens, launder your nightcloak?" He spoke with too much good humor.

"Find several apprentices and one large floater. You know where the ippicator skeleton sits in the caves. Collect the head and send it to m'Dame d'Embry. A gift to the Alliance from the Hoorka."

Cranmer whistled. "That's a princely gift, Ulthane. You of all people should realize what it's worth."

"It's a dead animal, scholar. Nothing more. It's worth nothing to Hoorka-kin. It belongs only to Neweden."

Cranmer hesitated, then nodded. He rubbed his hand over his forehead, smearing the ink. "As you wish, sirrah. I'll take care of it immediately, and I'll let Mondom know that you're on your way to her. Talk to you later, neh?"

"I'll have all the time you'll need."

"Good." Cranmer walked away, an off-key whistling echoing in his wake.

Gyll leaned against a wall as his thoughts lashed at him. To hear another person called "Thane" had struck him more deeply than he wished to admit. At least he was still Hoorka, he reminded himself, still of the kin.

He hoped it would be enough.

ABOUT THE AUTHOR

STEPHEN LEIGH has been selling short stories to SF magazines (ANALOG, ASIMOV'S, DESTINIES) since 1976. Although he has a Bachelor's degree in Fine Art and Art Education, he makes his living as a bass guitarist and singer for a couple of rock groups. He is married to Denise Parsley Leigh, who is an activist in SF fandom, and they presently live in Cincinnati, OH. *SLOW FALL TO DAWN* is his first novel and he is currently at work on the sequel.

He's a tough-guy detective living in a seedy 21st century America. He smokes hard and drinks hard and is certainly no soft touch when it comes to the ladies. More often than not, he's smack in the middle of danger—but he thinks on his feet and has a great nose for snooping. Catch Mathew Swain in his first three futuristic adventures:

HOT TIME IN OLD TOWN

When someone ices one of Swain's friends, Swain sets out to nail the killer. His relentless thirst for justice takes him to Old Town, a radiation-soaked mutant enclave where Swain uncovers a secret so deadly it's been paid for with a thousand lives. (#14811-7 • $2.25)

WHEN TROUBLE BECKONS (*on sale October 15, 1981*)

When Swain's rich friend Ginny Teal asks Swain to visit her on the moon, he's awfully reluctant. But Ginny sounds desperate and Swain gives in. But when he gets to the Moon, Swain finds Ginny out cold on the floor next to a dead body. (#20041-0 • $2.25)

THE DEADLIEST SHOW IN TOWN (*on sale February 15, 1981*)

Swain is hired for more money than he's worth to find a missing #1 newswoman and plunges deep into the dazzling world of a big video network, a ratings war and the misty borderline between reality and illusion that makes up the video of tomorrow. (#20186-7 • $2.25)

Read all three of these exciting Mathew Swain novels, available wherever Bantam paperbacks are sold.